THE LAST TO DIE

THE LAST TO DIE

KELLY GARRETT

sourcebooks
fire

Published by Sourcebooks Fire, an imprint of Sourcebooks
P.O. Box 4410, Naperville, Illinois 60567-4410
(630) 961-3900
sourcebooks.com

Originally published as *The Last to Die* in 2017 by Poisoned Pen Press.

Library of Congress Cataloging-in-Publication Data

Names: Garrett, Kelly, author.
Title: The last to die / Kelly Garrett.
Description: Naperville, Illinois : Sourcebooks Fire, 2019. | Originally
    published in Scottsdale, Arizona, by Poisoned Pen Press in 2017. |
    Summary: Thrill-seeking Harper Jacobs and her friends make a pact to
    engage in a series of break-ins from their own homes, but when Alex,
    looking to up the ante, suggests breaking into the home of a classmate,
    one of the group ends up dead.
Identifiers: LCCN 2019006134 | (pbk. : alk. paper)
Subjects: | CYAC: Mystery and detective stories. | Burglary--Fiction. |
    Stealing--Fiction. | Friendship--Fiction.
Classification: LCC PZ7.1.G376 Las 2019 | DDC [Fic]--dc23
LC record available at https://lccn.loc.gov/2019006134

Printed and bound in the United States of America.
VP 10 9 8 7 6 5 4 3 2 1

TO JIM

ONE

I'm about the same height as Sarah Dietz, with the same shoulder-length brown hair, so I knew no one would pay attention as I broke into her house.

It looked a lot like mine. Tan house on a large lot on a street of cloned homes. Her family was gone, or else they'd have the same black Lexus or BMW parked in front.

As soon I was through the front door, I pocketed Sarah's spare key. A few steps later and I was in front of the beeping alarm. 3-6-12. So easy, I didn't even need to write it down. Within seconds, the house was filled with silence.

House as tan inside as it was outside. Dark-brown leather

furniture in the living room off the foyer. Creamy brown walls. I turned into the office. Built-in bookcases. Lots of leather-bound books. A few golf trophies.

We'd agreed: we wouldn't steal anything that insurance and an AMEX card couldn't replace, so I ignored the golf trophies. Except. I pulled one of the golf clubs out of the mini hands of a golden golfer. It slid out, leaving the little man in midstroke without a club.

The three-inch gold club fit into the pocket of my black sweater. First score.

This was as easy as Sarah Dietz after she drinks a couple of beers.

SATURDAY NIGHT: APRIL 2

"More, Harper?" Alex didn't bother to wait for my response before he topped my glass with whiskey from his dad's stash, along with a splash of Coke.

"Good boy," I said. I propped my feet up on the edge of the navy-blue ottoman and sank back against the pillows of the matching couch in the Conways' basement. Alex put the bottles on a side table before crashing down next to me. The jolt caused me to spill my drink on my sweater.

"Sorry." Alex reached out to wipe the alcohol off my chest. I swatted his hand away and said in a purposefully bored tone, "Touch me again and I'll break your wrist." I looked away from him like he was an insect under my sneaker.

He put his hands up in mock surrender before leaning back. He put his arm on the couch back behind us, and I leaned away from him.

Paisley giggled from across the room where she knelt on the floor with Benji. He had a white cable in one hand as he tried to attach an iPad to the TV while Paisley looked over his shoulder like a fluffy blond-haired puppy in a flouncy polka-dot skirt. The curve of her hips and her tiny waist were perfectly accented by her tight white cardigan, like a pinup girl who had landed on the demure side of the retro calendar. Alex was checking her out, but her eyes were only looking at Benji. She giggled again, her blond hair brushing against his dark-brown hair.

"The mating cry of girls everywhere," Alex said. "The drunken giggle. A playful tap. You know what it's code for?"

"Just shut up and drink," I said. The whiskey burned a path from my throat down to my stomach as I sipped. I waited for it to burn through my fingers. My toes.

I glanced at my watch. Sarah had been gone for forty-five minutes. She should be back any minute, unless she'd decided to wimp out and not break into Gin's house. Maybe she'd gone home and was curled up underneath the covers of her bed, hoping we hadn't noticed she'd skipped out.

Gin. Saturday night would be a lot more fun if he were here instead of spring skiing with his family. I glanced back at Paisley and Benji, who were lounging in front of the TV, ice cubes clinking in Alex's glass next to me. Nerves flittered in my stomach. Was Sarah still in Gin's house? She better follow the rules.

"The show's primed to go!" Benji crowed and stood up, pulling Paisley along with him. She giggled again, and he stooped down to kiss her. Alex's knee bumped mine, and I jerked my leg away.

I took another sip of whiskey.

Paisley and Benji collapsed on the other side of the sectional couch as some episode of a web series overtook the TV and sound system.

"Pretty awesome sound, huh?" Alex said. He tried to stare into my eyes.

"Like I care."

"Took Benji long enough to set it up," Alex said, loudly enough for everyone to hear. "Good thing you weren't needed to rebuild the carburetor in the Chevy earlier today."

"Sorry I missed it. It would have been fun to work on it again with you and Uncle," Benji said, briefly looking at Alex but then glancing away. I glanced between them, so alike in many ways, with the same chocolate-brown hair and blue eyes. But Alex was definitely the alpha in their relationship. I glanced back at Alex, noting the smug smile smeared across his face.

"Did you get the Chevy running again? I love old clunkers," Paisley said.

"It's a '67 Chevy, not an old clunker," Alex said.

I held back a snort and Paisley gave me a sweet smile. She'd noticed Alex's dig toward his cousin. *Way to stand up for your boyfriend, Pais*, I said in my mind and held up my drink to her in a mock toast.

Alex was about to say something when there was a knock on the sliding glass door connecting the basement to the backyard. "Our girl is back!" Alex said as he sprang up and opened the door. Sarah sauntered in and struck a pose, raising a Louis Vuitton tote bag into the air. "Success!" She bowed, her hands brushing the floor as she leaned over.

Paisley and Benji clapped while Alex grabbed Sarah around the waist and gave her a big kiss. But as he let her go, his eyes found me. I gave him a sarcastic smile and took a gulp of whiskey.

"So how was your haul?" I asked. I kept my voice cool and unconcerned as I waited for her to brag she'd stolen something from Gin's room, just to mess with me.

Sarah upended the tote bag onto the ottoman in front of me.

Benji picked up a Rolex with diamonds on the watch face. "Good score!"

"I can't believe Gin's mom left that in plain sight in her bedroom." Sarah rolled her eyes dramatically as she spoke.

"Will we be able to pawn that? It's distinctive," I said, wondering why Gin's mother hadn't worn the watch on their ski trip. She had squealed when she opened it two months ago on her birthday and claimed it would never leave her wrist. Gin had nudged me with his hip and muttered in my ear, "Until my dad gives her something more blinged out."

Sarah knelt down and pulled a flash drive out of the mixture of drugs (Ritalin and Valium), a pair of platinum candlesticks, and a pearl-inlayed box about the size of a deck of cards. Nothing looked as expensive as the watch.

"What do you think is on this?" Sarah's face dimpled as she flipped the flash drive up in the air a few times. Her hazel eyes sparkled. "I found it in his dad's bedside table."

"That has to be irreplaceable," I said. My hands curled into fists.

We'd promised, back when we started the thefts, that we wouldn't steal anything that wasn't easy to replace. "There could be something important on that."

Sarah smirked at me. "They'll notice the burglary. Unlike some people."

I flinched and hoped the expression didn't flash across my face. My parents hadn't filed a police report or told their friends about our house being burglarized when we went to New Hampshire for my grandfather's funeral. But they'd noticed the theft.

They'd reacted to the theft.

They just thought they knew the culprit—and it wasn't me. Or Alex. Or anyone in my clique.

"I'll get my laptop from upstairs. Let's see what's on the flash drive." Alex's steps were steady even though he'd had several whiskey and Cokes. I looked back at Sarah, returning her defiant stare.

She glanced at the ground. "We can return it after we check it out," she said. Her eyes flicked to a framed photo of Alex and his dad on the wall. A smile blossomed over her face.

"Gin had some interesting photos of you in his room," she said.

Paisley gasped. "Harper! Did you and Gin take some special photos?"

A snort escaped from me before I had a chance to repress it. "No, Pais."

"I wouldn't have thought he'd be into forest green either," Sarah said. "I enjoyed his room. But you'd know more about it since you spend more time there than I do."

The ice cubes in my glass clinked as I took another sip, thoughts whirling through my mind. Sarah invading Gin's space rankled me, and I tried to figure out why. If Alex had gone into my bedroom when he burglarized my house, he hadn't left any signs or anything out of place. He'd emptied the liquor cabinet and broken the lock on my parents' medicine cabinet upstairs, clearing that out as well. He'd even stolen aspirin and over-the-counter cold medicine. He'd rifled through my mother's jewelry box, leaving most of it behind but snagging a few rings and a pair of diamond earrings.

But my room, and more importantly Maggie's, seemed untouched. Part of me knew Alex had snooped in my room. So I shouldn't be surprised Sarah had done the same. Although I'd ignored her bedroom when I broke into her house.

Paisley vibrated in place. "So what was the photo?" she asked.

A small smile crossed my lips. Of course she'd focus on the photo. "Sarah probably saw one of us after one of Gin's soccer games last year. It's a great photo." Maggie had taken it with her new phone and texted it to us immediately after and then emailed it. Then she printed it at a pharmacy and gave us both copies. Gin had framed his, while mine was on a bulletin board in my room.

A series of thuds told me Alex was on his way back to the basement. He set up his laptop on the bar on the far side of the room, and Sarah tossed him the flash drive. Benji joined him.

Paisley was saying something about her blog when Alex let out a loud chortle.

"Find anything interesting?" Sarah asked, and she slinked toward the boys, swinging her bony hips. Paisley and I followed.

Alex laughed. "Guess who sees himself as an amateur Larry Flynt?"

"The king of porn from that movie?" Paisley asked as Alex turned the screen in our direction.

I glanced at the scene and then averted my eyes. "I didn't need to see that!" I wanted to scrub the image of Gin's mother posing naked for the camera from my brain. Her fake assets were clearly displayed, as was the glittery watch on her wrist. Alex turned the screen back around to face him. "There are some folders labeled 'financial docs' too. Wonder if they contain more porn?"

"We need to take that back," I said. "Gin won't be cool with this."

"You mean you're not cool with this," Sarah said under her breath.

"Screw you." I faced Sarah, and she pivoted toward me with her shoulders straight. I stared at her, and she looked away after she'd made eye contact, reaching one hand up to twist the hair at the end of her ponytail.

"Girls! Let's get some Jell-O, or at least a camera, before you get into a girl fight," Alex said. "Are you sure you need to wear those sweaters if you fight? You should take them off first."

I shoved my temper back down inside me.

Alex moved next to Sarah and put his arm around her. She gave me a smug smile. "Harper's right," he said, and the smile vanished.

"About what?" Sarah asked.

"We do need to return this," Alex said as he looked into Sarah's eyes. "Since you took it, you should take it back."

"Only if you come with me." She gave him a flirty smile.

"You might be able to talk me into that," he said, and so she stretched up on her tiptoes and kissed him.

"We can re-create some of the photos," she whispered as they broke apart. She grabbed Alex's hand.

"See you freaks later." Alex pulled the flash drive out of his laptop before following Sarah out the door.

Paisley squealed as they left. "Do you think they're going to—"

Benji said no at the same time I said yes. Paisley laughed and twirled around. I imagined particles of whiskey swirling in the air around her.

"So creepy," she said.

"I guess it's a new place for them," Benji said. "They like to do it in weird places. Remember when the janitor almost caught them in the boys' room at school last month?"

"On that note, I'm going home," I said.

TWO

LATER THAT NIGHT

I propped my bike up against the side wall of the garage and quietly shut the door behind me as I entered the kitchen. The crisp night air hadn't obliterated the whiskey warmth tingling in my legs.

There was a light on in the breakfast nook. Crap. I told myself to walk steady and tall.

I wasn't drunk. Really.

My shoulders relaxed when I caught the glint of light bouncing off curly red hair. Maggie. I flipped the light switch, making the light go off briefly before turning it back on.

Maggie turned, and a smile spread across her face, lighting up green eyes just like the ones I see in the mirror every day. I paused for a moment. Her eyes seemed so innocent versus the reflection I'd seen staring at myself the past few years. I shook my head, telling myself I'd had too much to drink if I was drunk enough to think I'd ever felt as innocent as Maggie. "Everyone's asleep," she signed. Her hearing aids were on the table in front of her, next to a half-full cup of hot chocolate.

I nodded, and I signed back while also speaking out loud. "Why are you still up?"

"Don't feel like sleeping yet. We were arguing about a CI again."

"I'm sorry I wasn't here to run interference."

Maggie looked resigned, and I could imagine the discussion she'd sat through. It'd be the same as last week. My dad would say they didn't think she was a candidate for cochlear implants when she was a baby, but now she was. Of course she'd want to be able to hear, or at least have some sort of approximation of hearing. Maggie would argue that she was happy the way she was.

Except I hadn't been here to tell my father that Maggie was old enough to have a say in the surgery, and he'd yell at me to butt out.

"I told my doctor I didn't want the surgery. He won't go through with it unless I want it. Dad isn't happy." Maggie's jaw took on the determined set I recognized. It was the look she had when she'd decided she was going to throw out all of the blue crayons when she was five, and when she'd decided she was going to move all of my old Nancy Drew novels to her room when she was nine.

"You don't need to convince me, Mags. I'm on your side." Her shoulders relaxed, and she slumped back in her chair. She reached out and picked up her hot chocolate. "Hey, your nails are pink! That's a first."

"I thought Ella and I were just going out for pizza for her birthday, but her mother took us out for manicures too. My toes are purple." Maggie blushed slightly as she signed.

"I love it! Should we do something like that for your birthday next month? Or go back to that escape room place you loved? Think we could solve the puzzle in less than an hour again?" I sat down next to her at the table.

Maggie shrugged and looked down at the red place mat.

I motioned to get her attention. "What's up?"

"I wanted to go to the ice cream house with my friends from school for my birthday, but Mom thinks that's not big enough. She wants it to be memorable."

"Yeah, she went wacky over my thirteenth birthday too," I said. "Do you remember? We had that big pool party at the club."

"Didn't you do that last summer for your sixteenth?"

"Yeah, except my thirteenth was pool-and-pineapple-themed."

Maggie's whole face lit up. "That's right! I remember the pineapple cake. But why did you pick it? You hate pineapple."

"I've always hated it. I didn't eat any at the birthday party either," I said. "Someone handed me a slice of cake after I'd blown out the candles, and the sight of the pineapple slices on top made me gag."

"Harper..." Maggie trailed off.

"What?"

"Your signing is a little sloppy."

"Sorry, Mags."

"Are you drunk?"

"Nah, just had a little bit. Don't you worry about it."

"Daniel was over for a while tonight."

"I didn't realize he was out of rehab." I glanced over at the family portrait on the wall of the breakfast room. It was about ten years old. Three-year-old Maggie and six-year-old me were wearing matching pink dresses with flowers in our hair. Nine-year-old Daniel had a matching flower in the pocket of his charcoal gray suit, which matched our dad's. Mom's hair was curled over her shoulders. We all looked angelic. Perfect from the outside, polished. Like an apple secretly rotting from the inside out.

My attention snapped back to Maggie, who signed something for the second time.

"He was just visiting and making amends. Again. He went back. He has another three weeks. Or months. Three something."

"Then I'll just catch him next time he comes by to apologize."

"Harper!"

"Just kidding, Maggie. Maybe we can stop by and see him next week. I'm pretty sure they have family visiting hours. The last rehab place did."

She nodded at me. I gave her a quick hug after I stood up. "See you tomorrow, tiger. Don't stay up too late."

"Night." She turned back to her cocoa.

THREE

MONDAY MORNING: APRIL 4

"Hey, killer."

I didn't have to look around the door of my locker to know Alex was leaning against the expanse of gray metal running down the hallway.

"What's up?" I didn't bother with any sort of enthusiasm, not even to glare at the sophomore girl in an almost-too-short-for-the-dress-code khaki skirt giving Alex a shy smile as she walked by. His spine straightened slightly as he noticed, but otherwise he didn't react. He didn't push one of the curly strands of chocolate-brown hair off his forehead or flex his arm muscles like he did last year before he started hooking up with Sarah.

"You're looking good these days," Alex said. He eyed my fitted red button-down shirt where it fastened across my chest. I regretted stuffing my navy school cardigan onto the top shelf of my locker instead of wearing it.

"What do you want? And chill with the flattery. It won't get you anywhere." I shut my locker after shoving my U.S. history textbook into my bag.

"So I have an idea, and since you're the devious one in the group, I wanted to talk it over with you," Alex said. "Plus, flattery will get me everywhere. Got me out of a pop quiz earlier today."

"Coach Johnson's health class? Please."

"Nah, not his class. Ms. Erikson's English class. She practically swooned when I told her I was taking care of my sick mother instead of studying last night."

"Your mother moved away years ago!"

"Erickson's new and doesn't know that," Alex said. He had his I'm-king-of-the-school look on his face. He followed alongside as I walked toward my next class. His mother escaped town when we were nine and left Alex with his dad when she took a job in Panama. Or Peru. Some country that started with a *P*. She stops by every summer and sends a gift on his birthday.

"Really, let's talk." Alex shoved me into Coach Johnson's office, which was empty, even though the door was open. He followed me in and pulled the door shut behind him.

"I have to get to class. If I get detention, I'll be late for practice," I said. My soccer coach is serious about us being on time, and being late usually means being benched for the next game. There's no way I'd open the door to Sarah starting before me, even though our coach would pull her after a few minutes and put me in after he'd made his point.

"Don't worry. I know where Johnson keeps his excuse slips, and he signs them in advance. You're covered."

I sat on Coach Johnson's desk as Alex sat in his chair across from me in the small office. "Go for it. Although if I get in trouble, I'm taking you down with me."

"I would expect nothing less," Alex said. "So—my idea."

He glanced at the door and scooted closer to me. "We've hit up all our houses, right?"

"Yeah," I said.

"So we need a new challenge. Something more difficult than just entering our own homes," Alex said.

"We need to be careful," I said. "Someone's going to catch on. The police will connect the break-ins back to us. Eventually. Someone's going to figure out we're all friends."

"You've already been thinking about this." Alex sounded like he approved. "I've thought of that too. Which is why I have a new idea. Something that will throw suspicion off us."

I motioned for him to go on.

"We need new targets. Options not too close to us. But look around—we have plenty of leads."

"Explain." I crossed my legs at the ankle, and Alex leaned in so closely he touched my knee. "It's simple: let's find out who's going out of town and break in to *their* houses," Alex said. "If we listen, we can find new houses."

"Hmm." My legs brushed against Alex's shirt as I recrossed my ankles and leaned back against the desk. "You know, the girl whose locker is next to mine is going to Disney World next week. I know her locker combo—and she keeps a spare key in there."

"How do you know her combination?" Alex asked.

I shrugged. "She kept whispering it at the beginning of the school year. She's not very good with locks—she still has trouble opening it. She wanted to get her lock swapped out with a key. She's in my web design class and asked for next week's assignments so she won't fall behind."

"Do they have an alarm?"

"No idea. But we can always bolt if they do."

"Sounds like a plan," Alex said. "But we should up the ante a little bit. Steal some bigger items."

"But with the same terms."

"Do you mean only stealing replaceable things?" Alex turned his head slightly as he studied me.

"Yeah."

"For sure. Those are easier to fence anyway. Less distinctive. Unlike the stupid Rolex Sarah stole. Did you know those have registration numbers? I checked. It could be traced back to us, so I need to figure out how to off-load it."

I shrugged. "Put it in a donation box or something?" It's not like we needed the money, although it would buy a lot of beer. Since it was the off-season for Alex, and always the off-season for nonathletic Benji and Paisley, they could take something stronger without running the risk of failing a team drug test. Not that I did drugs, period.

"Nah, that'd be a waste. I'll think of something." He leaned in closer to me. "I'm taking some stuff from Sarah and Benji's hauls to pawn to the city tomorrow. You want to come?"

I shook my head. "Practice game against the B team."

"That's why I stopped playing soccer. You're bananas for playing year-round."

I shrugged. "The Earth would stop rotating if I quit." My father's if-you-quit-soccer-my-head-will-explode expression from when I brought up not playing spring soccer crossed my mind. I knew he wanted to be able to brag about his daughter getting a full athletic scholarship to school, and playing for the best club in the area, along with being a four-year high school starter, were the first steps.

"So when does what's-her-name fly to Florida?"

"Saturday morning."

Alex's smile was feral. "Then let's hit it up Saturday evening or Sunday. I'll text later, and we'll set something up."

"I'll need to get the key," I said, thinking of my weekend plans. I was supposed to take Maggie to her soccer game on Saturday morning. Other than that, the time spread out before me in a blank canvas. A project with Alex sounded like the perfect way to fill some time until Gin returned.

"Can you get it Friday afternoon after practice?" Alex asked. "After she leaves for the week?"

"We're practicing across town."

"Maybe you can leave a book behind and have to swing by? Doors don't lock until five, and, besides, you can always sweet-talk the janitor into letting you in again."

"I'll see what I can do," I said. "Now write me a pass so I can get into class."

"What's the rush?" his voice was a little husky.

I laughed. "Drop the Don Juan act and help me out. I need to do well in this class." I didn't add that history was actually my favorite. I even finished the reading ahead of time.

"If you insist." Alex's hand brushed my knee as he reached under and pulled open a drawer. He extracted a stack of yellow slips and filled out my name. He was right; Coach Johnson had already signed them.

"Here you go." As he handed me the slip, he gave me the same look I'd seen him give Sarah before, as well as countless other girls crushing on him. "Although, we could have some fun."

I stood up and pushed him backward. "Save it for someone else. Your charm doesn't work on me."

Alex gave me an exaggerated sigh and put his hands over his heart, but he stepped out of the way. I left the office without looking back.

LATER MONDAY EVENING

I'd left my laptop open on my desk and facing the bed. The icon for a video chat program popped up. I dropped my novel for English, which

I hadn't opened, although I'd stared at the front cover of hypnotic circles within circles for a while, and jumped across the bedroom.

I accepted the request from "SuperGin" and swiveled my laptop to face the other direction so I could sink down into the leather desk chair.

"Hey." Gin smiled at me from some ski resort in Canada. Light green walls behind him showed off his skin, permanently a few shades darker than my summer tan. A knit navy beanie covered his close-cropped black hair. A white headboard and a painting of a sunset adorned the wall behind him.

"Hey yourself. Having fun on the slopes?"

"You know it. Snowboarded from eight a.m. until they closed and kicked me off the mountain."

"Wish I was there." I smiled back at Gin, feeling as if the sun had just come out after a thunderstorm.

"Maybe I'll convince my parents to invite you next year." I laughed before being able to gasp out, "Good luck." I imagined Gin's dad's reaction to bringing his son's girlfriend to something he referred to as "family time." I'd long ago realized that was code for "no Harper."

"So how's it going? You piss anyone off since we last talked?" His eyes studied me, clearly expecting me to answer yes.

I relaxed into the chitchat, recounting my day to Gin, until he asked the question I'd been waiting for. I stiffened in my chair.

"So did Sarah do it?" He glanced around and relaxed slightly, like he was confirming he was alone.

"Yeah," I said. "She kept to the rules and returned your key and code to Benji. It's back in the box. So we're all good."

"What'd she take?"

"Well…" I picked up a pen from my desk and clicked it open and then clicked it shut.

"Come on, Harper, don't fail me now. Just say it." There was a serious note under a joking tone in Gin's voice, like he'd wanted me to bring this up ever since we started chatting. I put the pen down and picked up a pencil sharpener shaped like a robot and then put it down too. I took a deep breath and heard Gin take a similar breath on the other side of the connection.

"Your mother left her diamond watch behind."

"Fuck." He squeezed his eyes shut and tapped his head with the palm of his hand.

"Want me to return it? I can." I almost added, "Just like the flash drive," but I bit the words off before they exited my mouth. Gin didn't need to know we'd seen some *bam chicka bam bam* photos of his mom. I crossed my fingers under the desk, hoping he wouldn't work out that I was accidentally-on-purpose leaving something out.

Gin eyed me across our respective Wi-Fi networks like he knew I was leaving something out. "Maybe…"

My voice sounded slightly breathless as I broke in. "Alex still has everything. He said he was going to pawn it later this week. The rest of the stuff wasn't that big a deal. Some candlesticks. Small stuff."

Gin was silent. He sported a pensive look as he weighed his

options. I wished he was close enough to touch instead of having to talk across hundreds of miles.

"You're so good at the whole thinking before leaping thing… Sorry, didn't meant to say that out loud," I said.

Gin snorted. "Don't worry about the watch," he said. "It makes the burglary believable."

"You sure?"

"Yeah." He didn't sound sure to me, and he still looked tentative. I was about to call him out on it but then he said, "So, you have a game tomorrow, right?"

"Yeah, and Maggie's playing on Saturday. She might even start."

"Fantastic! Tell her—"

"Gordon, I need you. Now." Gin's mother's voice screeched through the speakers. She must have been standing on the other side of his laptop, because I could see her reflection on the wall like a shadow puppet show.

"Sorry, I have to go. See you Sunday?" He leaned in closer.

His face covered my entire screen.

"Of course." I said, even though Sunday was six long days away. "Let me know if you change your mind—" He winked at me and was gone.

I sighed, wishing we'd had our usual game of "No, you log off first." The heaviness surrounding me all day fell over me again like early morning fog. Should I really break into Marisa's locker, let alone her house? I should have asked Gin what he thought. He always sees things I miss.

Why was I worrying about this? It's not like we were hurting anyone. Look at what happened when my house was hit. Daniel would have gone back to rehab anyway. Granted, he hadn't stolen anything this particular time, but it's not like my parents would have trusted him again anyway.

It's not like he hadn't stolen from me before. Like the birthday and Christmas money I'd saved up when I was fifteen. The Vicodin from when I'd broken my arm. Besides, he needed to go back to rehab. He'd slid back into his world of hard-core drugs. It was inevitable.

Marisa's house was a challenge, and Alex had promised we wouldn't liberate anything her family couldn't replace.

FOUR

LAST FEBRUARY

Daniel's duffel was by the front door as I walked inside. It was the same bag he'd taken to rehab last time. The one my father bought for himself but didn't like. It was clearly perfect for his son's trips to rehab.

Maggie waved at me from the den. "He's going back to rehab," she signed.

"I figured that out," I signed back, not bothering to speak out loud.

"Daniel says it wasn't his fault. He didn't steal anything. But Mom and Dad don't believe him." Maggie's eyes were round and there might have been a few tears gathering at the sides.

"It'll be okay." I didn't tell my little sister I'd seen a plastic bag of white powder fall out of Daniel's coat pocket last week. And that the pupils of his eyes had been too large and unfocused a few days later. So even though he hadn't stolen this time—Alex had burglarized our house and used the key I made—it was inevitable. No reason to confess or feel guilty. It's not like Daniel wasn't rehab bound again anyway. My mother had already replaced the ugly silver knickknacks sprinkled around the house with even uglier, and more expensive, decorations. Her doctor had been so sympathetic about her Valium disappearing that he'd given her a new prescription.

"This is the last time we're sending you to get cleaned up." My father and Daniel were walking down the stairs. "This is it. If you fall off the wagon again and end up in the gutter, we won't help you back out."

I winced, and Maggie signed, "What?"

I shook my head at her. Nothing could convince me to translate that for Maggie. She didn't need to worry that she'd never see Daniel again. That he'd end on the streets, strung out, panhandling for money. Or worse.

They walked to the bottom of the stairs and turned into the foyer.

Wait, is that really Daniel? His sweatshirt had several stains and looked like he'd been living in it for days. He hadn't washed his hair for at least as long, and his face had scabbed-over scratches on one side. The eye on the non-scabbed side was covered in a bruise that had faded to a yellow brown.

So different from the brown-haired, green-eyed boy who'd drifted in the popular-but-not-too-popular crowd for most of his time at high school, getting good-enough grades to keep our parents off his back, but not good enough for them to brag. Sarah and Paisley had crushed on him majorly our freshman year. He'd quit soccer at nine and baseball at twelve. He'd gone on exactly one golf outing with our dad before forsaking golf forever.

There was only one thing he hadn't quit. Or rather, couldn't quit. Hence the third trip to rehab.

"We're leaving now," my dad said. Daniel picked up his duffel bag.

"Daniel?" I said. "Happy birthday. The big nineteen."

"Thanks, Harper. You're the only one who remembered."

His smile was a shadow of his former self. My father grunted. "We'll go get ice cream or something to celebrate when you get out." I put my arm around Maggie's shoulders.

"Sounds like a plan." He signed "See you later" to Maggie, and they left.

FRIDAY AFTERNOON: APRIL 8

Sarah was nattering on about something as we stretched during our soccer warm-up. I focused on my left ankle, which had been a little sore during my run yesterday. I didn't want to miss our next game if it decided to swell up.

Rain drizzled down on us as we ran some drills, then some laps, and then more drills, until finally my favorite part of practice arrived: scrimmaging. The time I could just play for a while. Even if the coach gave us instructions on what to focus on, like one-touch passes, it was a chance to just play and feel the flow of the game.

We broke into small three-a-side games across the field, with cones for goals. Sarah lined up on the other team. I smiled to myself; she was on the B team, but she was gunning to join the A squad next fall. One of her biggest obstacles? Me. I'd nailed down one of the starting center-mid spots years ago.

It didn't take us long to score our first goal. I slid a pass through two defenders for my teammate to one touch and knock between the cones.

For the first time all practice, I felt free. My teammate passed me the ball, and Sarah ran up to me to defend. I stepped over it, pulling it onto my right foot, and protecting the ball with my left leg.

Only to have Sarah kick my left ankle. Hard.

Twice.

"What the fuck are you doing?" I yelled at her. "Play the ball!"

"It was an accident." Sarah looked at her teammates, as if she expected them to back her up.

"Be careful. Kicking someone once happens. Twice isn't cool," one of them said in a quiet voice that clearly said, "Don't drag me into this, Sarah."

Sarah glared at me. "Diva."

I punched her. My fist connected with her cheekbone and the side of her nose. She jumped on me, grabbing for my hair. I pulled a handful of her ponytail, jerking her head back. She grabbed me as she fell, and I landed on top of her, my elbow digging into her chest.

She pushed at me and bit my arm. I punched her in the stomach and when she gasped, I rolled on top of her and swung my arm back to hit her again.

"What's the meaning of this?" Someone dragged me off her. Our goalie grabbed Sarah when she tried to come after me. She fought to come at me but couldn't break free.

"Explain," our coach said without letting go of my arm. I dared Sarah to come at me again with my eyes but didn't say anything out loud.

"Sarah kept hacking Harper during the scrimmage," a voice said from the side. Sarah was snorting as she breathed and strained forward against our goalie, who'd wrapped one long arm around Sarah's chest.

"So Harper yelled at her, and Sarah said something, and they started fighting. Sarah totally bit Harper's arm. Cannibal."

I continued to glare at Sarah while my teammates talked. Whispers surrounded us. A few giggles. I wanted to ram the comments down their throats. Right after I finished with Sarah. My breathing was hard, like I'd just sprinted at the end of a five-mile run.

"Sarah, go run laps," our coach barked out. "Harper, with me."

His fingernails dug into my shoulder through my jersey as he dragged me to the sideline. "What was that, Harper?" he growled.

I shrugged, the anger bubbling inside me. It wanted to erupt again. Preferably on Sarah in a massive explosion that would rock her world and teach her not to mess with me again. Ever.

"I want an answer."

"She kept kicking me in the ankle on purpose." I forced my anger back into a cage inside me, telling myself to take a deep breath. Pissing off Coach wouldn't help me right now.

"How do you know it was deliberate?" I could feel his eyes

staring at my face as I looked over his shoulder toward the playground in the park.

"Too many times in the same place, and she knows I did PT on that ankle after last season. Even if she was just out of control, she still deserved it." I looked back at Coach, making eye contact this time. My voice was more controlled and laced with seriousness, like I was positive I was in the right. It's not like I was the first person to get mad at Sarah for hacking, I reminded myself as I continued to stand tall against his laser beam of a stare.

Coach sighed. "Go run six laps. No meandering. Then go home. I see you punch someone again and you're off the team. Got it?"

I shrugged and turned to do my laps. Coach called Sarah over so we didn't pass each other, although she glared in my direction as she jogged across the field. Might as well get the laps over with quickly, especially since it meant I could leave for the day.

After all, when the laps were over, I had a project to finish. Some minor breaking and entering at school. A slow smile spread across my face, although it slipped into a grimace as I stepped on a rock and my ankle wobbled. I powered through the pain.

I started to look forward to breaking into Marisa's locker.

FIVE

FRIDAY AFTERNOON, CONTINUED

My teammates were still scrimmaging when I left. I waved. Part of me wanted a shower, as the rain had drenched my hair and soaked my long-sleeved shirt and short-sleeved jersey down to my sports bra. My feet squished inside my cleats. I pulled off my shin guards and tossed them onto the floor of the passenger-side seat along with my cleats before pulling on a pair of flip-flops.

After I parked in front of the high school, I pulled a wool cap over my drowned-rat hair and slid a dry sweatshirt over my soccer clothes. It would get wet from the inside out, almost as if I were sweating up a storm, but hopefully I wouldn't be inside long enough for it to matter.

It was 4:45, just fifteen minutes before my high school was

locked up for the day, according to Alex. The front door opened when I pulled on it.

So far so good. Although I kept waiting for someone to stop me and ask what I was doing at school so long after classes ended. Shouldn't it be obvious I wasn't supposed to be here?

I nodded at a couple of seniors I knew. They were dressed in shorts and T-shirts and carrying baseball gloves, so they must have had practice indoors. Lucky bastards. Baseball players never have to practice in rainstorms.

My shoes squeaked slightly on the ground when I turned the corner to enter the juniors' hallway. I told myself to walk with confidence as I strode toward my locker. I just stopped one past my usual spot. Locker 454 instead of my usual 453. I had slipped my black leather gloves on while I was still in the car. Hopefully, people would assume I was just cold. That would explain the slight shake in my hands. I told the butterflies in my stomach that no one would think I was nervous. I spun the dial of Marisa's locker. 55-13-44. It opened easily, showing me the photos Marisa had printed of the actors she said were hot. Ugh, she had terrible taste. I laughed to myself when I realized I'd scrunched up my nose at the photos. The top shelf of her locker was almost empty. Just a small bag she kept tampons in and an empty neon-orange water bottle. Then my fingers hit a piece of plastic attached to a piece of metal toward the back of the locker. Success. Her spare house key on a plastic key ring shaped like a cow.

I shut Marisa's locker, trying to keep my cheek muscles from pulling my mouth up into a grin. One just doesn't go around with an idiotic smile splashed across one's face for no reason. Especially after committing a crime.

The key chain slid easily into my sweatshirt pocket. My fingers itched to text Alex to let him know I'd been successful. Sarah was going to flip tomorrow night when she heard about the plan.

Really, how do criminals mess up? This was so freaking easy.

"Ms. Jacobs?"

I paused when I heard my name spoken in a low voice. I turned to see Principal Jeffries at the corner where the north and east hallways met. I'm pretty sure he uses a ruler to trim his black mustache every day.

"Yes?"

"What are you doing here?"

"Oh, just had to get something from my locker. Homework for English." I motioned to the Adidas bag over my right shoulder. I'd tucked *The Bell Jar*, the novel we'd just started in English, inside just in case.

"If you're not practicing with a sports team, or at a club meeting, you need to be off school grounds." He glanced back down the hall behind me.

"Just going now." I forced a bright smile to cover my lips. "I'll remember that in the future."

"Be sure you do." I could feel him watch me as I walked down the corridor. Another layer of cold seemed to settle over me, like the dampness of my clothes was slipping into my skin. My heart thumped in my ears as my whole body started to shiver.

I really needed to get home to change. I slipped my fingers back into my pocket and pulled out the cow key chain.

Really? A cow? Although come to think of it, Marisa's brown eyes are flat. The same brown as Gin's but not nearly as lively or soulful.

A piece of Scotch tape on the back rubbed against my finger so I turned it over. Black lettering on the back read *Home 2873*.

I laughed and felt a little warmer.

Marissa had written her alarm code on her house key. Could this get any easier?

SIX

SATURDAY MORNING: APRIL 9

Maggie offered me a bowl of oatmeal as I entered the kitchen, and I nodded yes. She fixed it how I like it—with only butter and salt—and brought it with her into the breakfast room. Her oatmeal was covered in honey and milk. She swirled her spoon through it.

"You have everything ready for the game?" I asked, and she nodded in response. She was already dressed in her dark green uniform with a shamrock on the chest. I didn't have to check if she was already wearing her shin guards. She always put them on first thing in the morning on a game day for luck. Maggie was practically vibrating in place, getting ready for the game, as she tried to eat. I knew how she felt: the jangle of nervous energy, the jittery thoughts you have to focus down into a concentrated effort. I felt something similar when I thought of my upcoming burglary.

The steady pounding of dress shoes on tile made me turn my head slightly. My father was dressed in a suit instead of his usual Saturday morning golf attire. I waved at him.

"Has anyone made coffee?" he grumbled, and I turned back to my oatmeal. He swore and started opening and shutting cabinets, pulling out a box of coffee pods. "Would it kill anyone to make a pot of real coffee when they wake up?"

I touched Maggie lightly on the arm and gave her a sympathetic smile. Her nervous expression closed off into a straight face. I didn't bother reminding him that Maggie was too young to drink coffee, and I only drank espresso drinks when I was out. Usually because Gin bought one for me when we studied.

"Have you talked any sense into her?" Dad was unwrapping a protein bar as he spoke. The coffee maker was blinking a red staccato light as it warmed up.

"Nah, I think Mom still likes Prada best." I turned back around, showing my back to him.

"You know what I'm talking about."

I turned again and looked at him. "Maggie's right here. You can try talking with her. But she knows what she wants."

Maggie touched my arm and signed at me. "What's going on?"

I signed back. "Nothing. Eat your breakfast."

"What'd you say to her?" The light had switched to green, so he started brewing coffee, his fingers fidgeting against the counter as he waited.

"I told her to eat her breakfast. She has a game later this

morning. Not that you'd remember." I signed as I spoke, leaving the last sentence out. Maggie looked suspicious, like she knew I wasn't telling her everything, as she took a bite of oatmeal.

"Tell her good luck and I'm sorry I have to go the office instead of being there." He removed his stainless steel travel mug from the coffee maker before picking up his leather briefcase from the stool next to him.

"Do it yourself. Even better, you could try going to one of her games."

He gave an audible sigh and then put everything back down. "Maggie," he waved at her, and I nudged her and motioned toward him.

"Good luck," he said and clumsily signed. His hands quit moving as he faltered, making the wrong sign when he meant to say "luck." He partially turned away as he mumbled, "I'm sorry I can't go to the game today."

"Thank you," Maggie said out loud.

He nodded and then picked up his stuff and left. Once he was gone, Maggie signed to me: "What did he say after good luck?"

"That he's sorry he can't attend the game."

I picked up my now-empty bowl and carried it to the sink. The box of unused coffee pods was sitting on the counter, along with a jar of sugar, so I put those away before shoving my bowl in the dishwasher.

"Jerk." I was thankful for once that Maggie couldn't hear me.

A caramel latte was warm in my hands as Maggie and her teammates went through their pregame routine, and the bench of the middle row of the bleachers was cold against my legs, although the spring sun overhead promised to burn some of the chill out of the air. I glanced behind the bleachers of the soccer field toward the trail that led up a hill, through some trees, in the direction of the children's playground at Dry Hollow Park. Part of me wished I'd brought my gear to take a run on the system of trails winding through the park, although it would have crushed Maggie if I'd left her game. This summer. We'll come back and I'll lead her on a few jogs when it's sunny.

"Hey, killer," a voice said as a butt settled down on the bleacher next to me. I didn't have to turn my head to know it was Alex.

"What are you doing here?" I kept my eyes on the field.

"Pickup basketball," he said. "Although it's sad when it's little girls playing soccer instead of chicks like you improving the scenery."

I rolled my eyes. "Give it up."

Alex's leg bumped mine. "You ready for tonight?"

"Yeah, 'cause hanging out with Paisley and the gang takes so much prep time." I gave him a look that said, "Cool it. We don't need to attract any attention."

The cocky smile he gave me in return made me want to knock him off the bleachers. Tonight. I hid a smile. The nerves jangling around inside me, I decided, were excitement. Anticipation. Sweet, sweet anticipation.

SEVEN

SATURDAY NIGHT

"Isn't Gin back yet?" Paisley asked as we walked down the stairs to Alex's basement.

"Tomorrow," I said. "His flight lands sometime in the afternoon."

"Are you going to meet him? If Benji left for over a week, I know I'd have to meet him at the airport. I don't know how I'd survive for that long without seeing him." She made eyes that reminded me of the cow from Marisa's key chain as she looked across the room at Benji, except the color was wrong. He and Alex were looking at something together; their similar builds and identical coloring made them look like bookends. Benji snorted loudly and punched Alex on the shoulder.

"You'd probably live just like you did before you started dating," I said. "Remember when you dated that one guy our freshman year? What was his name? Silas?" I still had photos on my hard drive of Paisley sitting in Silas's lap at a party, a can of beer in one hand while her other hand was tangled in his hair. Benji had stared at them for months, jealousy clearly written across his entire body. He must have thought it was his lucky day when Silas was kicked out of the Academy for cheating and sent to some tough-love boarding school.

Paisley shook her head, causing her fluffy blond ponytail to whip from side to side. I stepped back so I wouldn't get her hair whipped in my eye. "Don't talk about Silas! I haven't thought about him in forever. At least a year," she laughed. "And don't try to change the subject. You're so stoic, but you know you miss Gin."

"If you say so." I dumped my empty backpack down next to the doorway and dropped my black peacoat on top. My mother bought me the coat for my grandfather's funeral last year. I smiled to myself when I wondered what Mom would say if she knew I was using the jacket to further my life of crime.

"Should we go see a movie or something?" Paisley asked. She twirled a lock of her hair around her finger like she always did when she was bored.

"Nah, I have a plan," Alex said. He looked around the room, watching how everyone reacted to his announcement. Benji snapped to attention.

"Ohhh, what?" Paisley perked up. Sarah joined us from her spot across the room, although she edged away from me. I smiled to myself; did she think I'd punch her again? I owed her a solid blow to the solar plexus, preferably when she didn't expect it. I gave her a feral smile.

Benji tilted his head when he looked at Alex, the way a dog does when he sees something interesting. It was the same look Alex had given me the other day. The head tilt must be a family thing, coded deep into their shared DNA.

"Well, it doesn't quite involve all of us." He smirked in my direction. "So here's the plan..."

I tuned out as he mentioned Marisa's house, key, *blah blah blah*.

"So who's going?" Benji asked. "You?"

"I'm thinking two of us should go this time."

"So me and you." Sarah flipped her hair over her shoulder and then smiled at me. A smile almost as cocky as Alex's usual expression. I gave her a half smile in return, just waiting for her expression to do a one-eighty. I'd give Alex the honors so I could watch her implode.

"Nah, just me and Harper," Alex said.

"What?" Sarah screeched. "Are you kidding me?"

"Harper got the key. She earned it. She figured out the target. You can go with Gin next time." Alex sounded like he was patting Sarah on the top of the head. I smiled openly; this was better than me punching her in the gut. The pain would last longer.

"Are we sure this is a good idea?" Benji asked.

Alex laughed. "Of course. We'll scout out easy targets. It'll be fun. Maybe we should have a getaway car just in case. Benji, you want to drive?"

Benji nodded like he was a getaway driver every day. "Of course."

Alex glanced at Paisley. "You and Sarah should stay here. We don't want too many people in the area."

"You sure? We could have multiple getaway drivers! Or if I was in the car with Benji, we could, like, make out if we saw anyone looking at us. So we wouldn't look suspicious."

"You'd just look horny," I said.

"Come on, Harper. You only YOLO once," Paisley said.

I burst out laughing. Paisley blinked at me and raised her eyebrows at Benji when he started laughing as well.

"This is stupid," Sarah said. "I'm not hanging around for this."

"Be a good sport," Alex told her. My smile mocked her.

"Sarah?" Alex said as his girlfriend started to stomp up the stairs.

"What?" The tone of her voice made me think she hoped Alex was telling her to stop and that she'd get her way. She wanted to be the one to break into Marisa's house with Alex. I wondered what was more important to her: keeping me away from spending one-on-one time with her boyfriend or from breaking into Marisa's house. I suspected the former. As if I'd let him into my personal bubble. I'd need industrial skank remover to get the smell of him off me.

"Remember, you can't turn us in. You can't tell. Unless you want to get thrown under the bus for breaking into Gin's house." Alex's voice was cold.

"Maybe I'll return the stuff I stole first." Her retort sounded petulant, like the way I talked to my father when I was twelve.

"Good luck since we already pawned it," Alex said.

"Asshole." Sarah's stomping feet turned into the sound of the front door slamming.

"Maybe Paisley should sit in the car with you, Benji. But maybe she should just stay here. You two decide if Paisley wants to take the risk," Alex said. He then eyed me. "You ready?"

I snorted. "I was born ready, jackass."

We left Paisley and Benji almost three blocks away parked in a dark spot. An entrance to the neighborhood trail system was maybe fifty feet away from their car, and we took the trail part of the way to Marisa's house. Then we walked a block on the sidewalk to reach the Forets' house, since the trail didn't run behind it. My heart thumped in a marching rhythm faster than our steps.

Marisa's family hadn't left their porch light on, which was a definite faux pas in neighborhood etiquette. Everyone else leaves their lights on. Every night. Except maybe Halloween and only then if you're one of those weirdos who doesn't give out candy. Or if you go out of town on the best holiday of the year.

Focus, Harper. After a few more steps, I was close enough to grasp the screen door handle and rotate it. Another step and I was up to the front door while Alex held the screen door open. A few seconds later and we were inside. Three steps and I was in front of the beeping alarm. Four quick taps of the keypad and the alarm was silent. Thank God Marisa had the right alarm code on her house key. I slid the key chain back into my pocket, even though the cow dug into my hip bone.

"So where should we start?" Alex asked as he flicked on the hall light and we were bathed in dim energy-efficient lights that promised to shine brightly. Eventually.

"You sure we should turn lights on? The neighbors have to know they're out of town."

"Good point!" The lights flicked off. Had he been this brilliant when he burglarized my house?

To the left was the office, with a living room to the right. I stepped down two steps into the office, remembering the golf trophies in Sarah's house. There wasn't anything as fun in this room, just books. No computer on the pine desk. Built-in shelves faced the windows to the front yard, but it was too dark for me to read the titles of the books.

"I'm heading upstairs," Alex said.

"Be careful with your flashlight," I called out after him. I paused by a diploma on the wall, squinting in the dark to read it. Masters in social work. Whatever.

I passed into the living room, careful to keep my flashlight off until I was in a room that didn't face the street. I didn't want to send up a strobe light that called out "Hey, look! Someone is burglarizing the Forets' house!"

The living room window faced out onto the street, so I ignored it and headed back to the kitchen and family room area facing the backyard. Same layout as my house, and Gin's, although it was smaller.

I ran my flashlight over the bookcase in the kitchen nook. A whole shelf of books on baking. *1,001 Soup Recipes.* Like you need a so many recipes you don't have to repeat a soup for almost three years.

A wooden sign, really just letters cut out of a block of wood that said *Family* was on the top shelf, painted black. I rolled my eyes as I pulled the sign off the shelf and stuck it in my backpack.

The cut-out letters weren't worth anything, but it was annoying. So dorky and faux inspirational.

The family room had giant oversized couches and fake-retro signs advertising Coca-Cola for five cents.

"Speaking of drinks…" I muttered to myself. A quick scan of the room showed me the most likely target. Waist-high cabinet painted bright red to match the fake signs. I knelt down in front of it, putting my flashlight on the ground as I pulled on the door.

Locked.

The flathead screwdriver from the front pocket of my backpack fit easily into my hand as I wedged it between the doors and twisted. A few quick pushes and turns and I'd broken the lock. It was a cheap, flimsy cabinet. I bet Marisa breaks in all the time.

Bingo.

Two wine bottles, the two-dollar cheap stuff, was inside, along with half a bottle of whiskey. "Why did they bother to lock this up?" My voice cut through the otherwise silent air. I nestled the wine in my bag anyway, using the wooden sign to keep the bottles from clinking against each other.

The discount whiskey remained by itself, visible through the broken door.

There wasn't much else worth stealing. Nothing valuable. I headed upstairs, noticing photos of Marisa, her little sister, and parents on the way up. Most of the photos involved camping or birthday parties with—I paused and moved in closer to the photo, angling my flashlight so the glass wouldn't reflect back into my eyes—homemade cakes. At least for Marisa's third birthday. No self-respecting bakery would send out a cake with those misshapen lumps.

I paused. Still, Marisa looked happy with her dopey smile next to the candle with the number three on it. Her pigtails were tied to the sides of her head with ribbon, and she wore some sort of pink smock. Very different from the elaborate party dresses found in all of my childhood birthday photos. Upstairs wasn't too exciting. Marisa's room was painted pale blue, and her furniture was all white and basic. Her little sister's room was pink with lots of ruffles. So boring. I gave each a quick glance but didn't bother going inside.

"Find anything good?" I asked Alex as he exited the master bedroom.

"Nah, crappy haul tonight," he said, heading downstairs. "You find anything in the dining room?"

"Just some cheap booze," I said, and stepped into the hall bathroom. There was only generic Tylenol in the medicine cabinet and cheap makeup from the drugstore. The same stuff Sarah, Paisley, and I had played with in middle school until Sarah's mom took us shopping for real makeup.

"Harper!"

I stepped into the hallway. "What?"

"If you break a window from outside, the glass ends up inside, right?" Alex asked.

"Obviously." Too many basketball drills must have scrambled his brain.

"I'll shatter the window by the door so cops will think this was a regular break-in."

Alex clearly spent a lot of time planning this. Of course we should do something before we leave to hide our easy entry. I'd planned on just leaving the door unlocked and the alarm off, like maybe the Forets had forgotten the basics on their way out of the house. But if Alex wanted to break a window, we could.

I shone my flashlight into the master bedroom. The light didn't show anything worth stealing, just basic white furniture and a small jewelry box that I was prepared to bet only contained costume jewelry. But I should check.

The sound of shattering glass from below me made me freeze.

"Oops, I should have waited until you were outside to break the window!" Alex laughed as he yelled. "Also, run!"

The alarm started to blare.

EIGHT

SATURDAY NIGHT, CONTINUED

I ran downstairs, tripping over the stairs on the way down. My gloved hand slid along the banister as I kept myself from falling head over heels.

Alex was gone. He'd left the front door wide open, and the window by the door was busted inward, with shards of glass covering the entryway. Lights turned on across the street and I knew someone had to be looking this way.

Crap. I ran to the back door and into the backyard. I sprinted across the lawn and vaulted over the fence, praying the house was on the trail system, after all.

No such luck. I ducked against the fence, thankful the lights were off in this house. I scurried across the backyard until I was up against the house. I practically hugged it as I inched toward the street, in time to see a police car drive by with its lights on, but no siren. A dog barked inside the house, but no one flipped on a light or shouted for Fido to shut up.

Crap. Adrenaline coursed through my body and I wanted to run, but I told myself to think. Be methodical. Don't do anything stupid to get caught. If you get caught, you can't kick Alex in the balls for breaking a window.

The house next door was dark, so I climbed the fence and jumped into their yard. I worked my way across the yard, coming up to another fence.

But the lights were on in the next house, and a man walked out of the back door and across the backyard, looking in the direction of the shrill alarm screaming from Marisa's.

I slunk alongside the house on the opposite side of the yard from the backyard with the neighbor, and this time the street was empty. No cars. No people. Hopefully, everyone's attention was on the Forets' street a block away. I pulled off my gloves and hat and shoved them into the backpack as I crept along the shrubs to the sidewalk.

Stand straight, shoulders proud. There's nothing inside my bag that screams "thief." It's not like I've never walked around the neighborhood with wine in my backpack before. I walked down the sidewalk toward Benji's car like I owned the world. Shoulders straight. No slouching. A quick—but not too fast—walk down the block, and two blocks down the trail, and I was almost back to the car. I made myself take slow, deep breaths. Be calm. Be cool.

"Boo!"

I jumped when a figure hurtled at me from the trees. I kicked at it, only for the figure to jump away and laugh before my black boots made contact.

"Gotcha, Harper."

"You're an ass, Alex. I should kill you right now."

He laughed. "Exhilarating, right? Want to do that again?"

"Exhilarating? I felt like I had to run for my life. That was not cool." I took a few more deep breaths, willing my heart rate to slow.

"Want a hug to make it all better?"

"Fuck you."

"C'mon, Benji and Paisley are waiting for us." Alex gave me one last glance over his shoulder as he walked away. "And Harper? Remember to return Marisa's key. Unless you think she won't notice it missing out of her locker."

My steps slowed. I knew I should speed up, rejoin Paisley and Benji, retreat into the safety of the car. Get away from here to someplace I had a reason or right to be. It's not like I could magically create a party I could claim I was walking to. But something tickled the back of my mind, competing with the mix of adrenaline and anger flowing through me. My hands clenched and I wished I'd stuck with the karate classes I'd taken in elementary school so I could kick Alex's ass properly.

"You're a douchebag for breaking the window when I was upstairs."

He turned to look at me. "Great way to up the ante, wasn't it?

You didn't leave fingerprints, did you? The police might take this break-in more seriously."

He turned and walked away.

My feet sped up when I realized something: I didn't have to beat Alex up to get revenge. I just had to think of something that would inflict maximum damage and make him fall onto his knees and beg for mercy.

NINE

The chirp of my phone distracted me from reading the most recent entries on Paisley's blog. She was extolling—her word—the virtues of faux-leather boots. *Meet at park?*

Gin. He was back. I smiled, wanting to dance, except I was still sitting on my bed. *Now?*

His response beeped seconds later. *Totally.*

C U soon. I tossed my tablet on my pillow and jumped off my bed doing a fake ballerina twirl before grabbing my jacket. Gin was finally home. The park was just two blocks away and halfway between our houses. It wasn't much of a park; just a block of verdant grass, sprinkled with picnic tables, with a play structure on wood chips in one corner. The real park, the see-and-be-seen place for families of the neighborhood association, had a crystal clear blue swimming pool and giant play area. But it was always busy.

Not like the minipark. Sometimes we'd see moms and kids from the surrounding houses, but it was usually quiet.

Another person entered the park at the same time I did. The walk gave him away, the even stride, even before I could make out his features, which I knew almost as well as my own. Brown eyes. Ski-jump nose that was the only thing he inherited from his mom. Black hair trimmed short or else it would erupt into a giant Afro. An image of Gin as a five-year-old flashed into my mind. We met at this park when his parents moved into the neighborhood. Our nannies knew each other and arranged a lunch date. Gin had been fascinated by Maggie's signing and was willing to race me from the picnic tables to the swings.

I did an exaggerated step-shuffle, and Gin mirrored the movement. My heart felt lighter, like I'd been missing something this past week. We met at our usual picnic table. Our initials were carved into the bottom. Gin had chosen a spot out of sight since the neighborhood association had zero tolerance for graffiti. Plus, it'd be easy to trace our initials back to us. It was nice to know they were secretly there, hidden from view. As Gin said, it was our private example of how all sorts of things were hidden beneath the surface if you cared to look. "I brought you something." Gin handed me a small paper bag with a gift shop logo stamped on it. I opened it to find a Whistler key chain.

"Thanks. My keys will love the change in style." But I gave Gin a smile so he wouldn't know I was being completely sarcastic. "I like that it's also a bottle opener. It's useful, not just pretty."

"Kind of like you."

"Ha-ha," I deadpanned.

"I think we need to talk." Gin's tone was hesitant. Like he was afraid I'd freak out on him. He sat down on the top of the picnic table with his feet on the bench. He stared across the park toward the swing set and tan houses on the other side of the street.

"What?" I sat down next to him. Was he breaking up with me? The thought sunk down into my stomach like I'd swallowed a balloon filled with marbles. Gin had never asked me if I'd be his girlfriend; it just happened. He'd always been my default, my best friend. He didn't have to ask me to homecoming, and I didn't have to ask him to Sadie Hawkins. I assumed we'd spend weekend nights together. We studied at each other's houses. Gin came to Maggie's soccer games with me if he could. He always planned something just for the two of us for my birthday, and I always sneak cookies into his locker for his.

We kissed on a regular basis. He was my boyfriend, even if I didn't spend time elaborating on what it meant. Like our parents assumed. Like everyone said. Can you break up with someone if you've never said out loud that you're boyfriend and girlfriend? Although I'd heard Gin refer to me as his girlfriend before.

"So—the whole housebreaking thing—I'm not sure if I'm down with it anymore."

Okay, not breaking up with me. My shoulders slumped slightly before I remembered breaking into Marisa's house last night. "What do you mean?"

"It was sort of fun to break into each other's houses. Exciting. But I felt weird after I did it, like I was violating my neighbors. I'm really not sure about doing it again."

"Same rules apply. We didn't steal anything unreplaceable," I said.

"Irreplaceable," Gin said.

"Whatever, Mr. SATs." Maybe he didn't know about Alex breaking out the window and setting off the alarm when I was upstairs. Had Alex told anyone about it? In retrospect, the adrenaline rush had been incredible. Not that I hadn't wanted to kill Alex at the time. Not that I still didn't want to plan out a particularly spectacular revenge. Something that punctured his overinflated ego.

"Benji and I talked about it, and he's not sure about this either."

"When did you talk to Benji?" Wasn't I supposed to be the first person he talked to after he got back?

"On the phone last night. Paisley and Alex were drunk, and he wanted to talk to someone sober enough for a serious conversation. He said you'd already bailed and he couldn't imagine calling Sarah after she stormed out."

"He didn't say anything last night when he heard the plan."

"Sounds like it was sprung on him without any chance for him to object." Gin stared straight ahead. His face could have been carved from stone.

I sighed. "Check yourself before you wreck yourself," I muttered.

"Exactly." Gin turned to me, and the stone like expression on his face softened. "I don't want you to get into trouble. Or me, for that matter. It'd derail our college plans. Felonies will do that to a person."

"Is it really a felony?" I asked.

"I'm pretty sure it is," Gin said. "I thought about asking my dad, but he'd have too many questions for me if I did."

"I'll think about this. All of it," I said. The toe of my red Converse sneaker had a black smudge, and I rubbed it against the bench in a swirling pattern.

"That's not all," I said.

"What's that?" Gin's eyebrows rose as he looked at me.

"Something else happened. When I was upstairs, Alex turned the alarm back on and then broke a window on purpose. I had to run out the back door and find my way back to Benji's car while staying out of sight of the neighbors. And the police."

"What?" Gin grabbed my lower arm. When I looked at him with raised eyebrows, he rubbed a gentle circle on my arm.

"You heard me."

"On purpose?"

"You heard me."

Gin let go of my arm and ran his hand over his head. "I can't believe he tried to throw you under the bus."

"I'm sure he didn't think I'd get caught."

"You could have been." Gin's voice was all cold fury. He stared into the distance, and a muscle in his jaw clenched.

"Let's not worry about that right now. It's done. We can't change it." My voice was equally grim.

"We'll need to tell Alex, together, that we're out. He's not going to be happy," Gin said. "Not that I care."

"Is Benji quitting for sure?"

"He will, and Paisley will follow, if we do."

"Let's talk tomorrow at lunch on how to break the news to Alex," I said. Gin's brown boots looked new and bigger than I remembered. My feet looked tiny next to his. Maybe Gin was going to grow a few inches taller. He was already seven inches taller than me at six feet even.

Gin scooted closer and put his hand on top of mine. His fingers spilled over the side, touching my jean-clad thighs. His voice dropped deeper and sounded smoky. "Quit with me. It'll be good. We'll find better things to do."

I looked at him, and he kissed me.

"Did I tell you I missed you?" he said when we came up for air.

"I'm sure you were pining for me every minute you were away."

Mom was sprawled out on the living room sofa with an issue of *Departures* in one hand and a mostly full glass of red wine in the other. An open bottle was on the table next to her, along with a bowl of grapes. I didn't know she ate grapes that hadn't been fermented first.

"I want to go to a yoga retreat in Malibu," she slurred and waved the magazine at me. "And I need a new ice cream maker. Cuisinart."

"Good for you. Where's Maggie?"

"Her friend texted and invited her over for dinner. Did you hear about Gin's house?"

I paused in the doorway of the room. Instead of heading upstairs, I stepped back into the room, wondering what the neighborhood gossip network had come up with. "No, what about Gin's?"

"They were burglarized when they were skiing!" Mom whispered, as if this was a big secret we needed to keep away from the neighbors.

I sat down on the edge of a blond leather wingback chair. "Really? Tell me more."

"Well, they didn't notice at first. But then Denise realized her god-awful watch was gone, so they started looking around more closely."

"Wow."

Mom sighed loudly and stretched before taking a sip of wine. I was about to stand up when she said, "Add that to the burglary on the other side of the neighborhood and man, this place is going downhill."

"Oh, there was another break-in?"

"Oh, yes, at the Forets'…"

She went off into full detail of everything that went down at Marisa's house, including the broken window.

"The police must have *just* missed the robbers! I heard they don't have any leads, but there were fingerprints left all over the house."

Hmm, I'd worn gloves. Black leather that fit snugly. Alex had joked about his driving gloves before we entered, so he couldn't have left any fingerprints behind either.

Alex. He's going to pay for breaking that window. My stomach muscles tightened, and I had to breathe out before I could get my fists to unclench.

"Did you hear this from gossip, or do you know Marisa's mom?"

"Oh, you know Marisa?" my mom said. "She's not a soccer player. Is she a regular in detention?"

"I know people who don't play soccer. And I'm not in detention that often," I said.

"Her mother used to be in my gardening club, but she works and couldn't make the meetings when we switched to Thursday afternoons. She has to work full-time to pay for Marisa's school fees." Mom waived her hand at me, knocking her wineglass over in the process. "Damn it!" she jumped up and overbalanced. She grabbed her napkin off the table and tried to sop up the wine on the couch.

"I'll get a towel and some club soda."

"Thanks, sweetie."

"Good thing I'm used to cleaning up your messes," I grumbled as I left the room.

TEN

We hadn't had a chance to tell Alex we were done, and I'd only caught a glimpse of him in school on Monday. He'd winked at me, making me want to retaliate by kicking him in the shins. But I'd promised Gin I'd be cool. Although the thought of the look on his smug face when we told him we were out made me smile.

One more class and then it would be time. We were meeting at Gin's as a group.

My feet slowed as I approached my locker and saw the figure standing next to it. Fat tears rolled down Marisa's face as she stood by her locker before our final class of the day. I glanced at her as I swapped textbooks between my locker and bag.

She hiccupped. "Do you have any tissues?"

"Umm…" I wanted to tell her to shove her tears where the sun doesn't shine, but instead I handed her a packet of tissues from my locker.

"Thanks."

"Fail a test?" I asked. Last time I'd seen Marisa bawl it'd been when she failed an algebra exam. Again. During her second year of the same math class. The one I'd passed in the eighth grade.

"No." Marisa blew her nose loudly, causing my whole body to cringe. "It's been a bad few days. We had to come home from Disney World early because someone broke into our house. My parents planned the vacation for years."

"That sucks."

"They stole my favorite CD. *The Veg at Warrior Rock.*"

I turned to face my locker and reached inside like I was looking for something to hide my smile from Marisa. Really? The Veg? They're horrid. Alex must have taken that. I wouldn't have touched it. A CD? Who buys them anymore? All of my music is on my laptop, tablet, or phone.

"Do you want the rest of this pack back?" Marisa offered the yellow-and-orange packet back to me.

"Nah, you keep it."

"You're so sweet." She tried to shove the package into the pocket of her khaki skirt. When it stuck, half in and half out, she looked down at her leg.

"And I have a run in my favorite scarlet tights!" She broke into fresh tears.

Good thing she kept the package of tissues. "I'm sure things will get better," I said. I debated patting her on the pink-button-down-covered shoulder, but instead I grabbed my leather backpack, closed my locker with a definitive thump, and walked down the hallway. I could feel the spring in my step, but then a stray thought took hold in the center of my mind.

What about this made me happy? Why would I celebrate Marisa's misery? What had she ever done to me, except annoy me with peppy hellos? Her stupid tights? The high-pitched giggle? Had her family really planned this vacation for years? Marisa hadn't talked about traveling before and the girl talked about everything, like spending her summer weekends camping with her family.

My steps slowed. When I thought of the burglaries, had I really felt happy? Joyful? Or had that sense of satisfaction come from a different place?

I remembered the simplicity of Marisa's house. No designer anything. Basic furniture in one of the smallest houses on the block, like her family didn't have a ton of money. Her mother worked, unlike my mother and Gin's. My mother had rambled that Marisa's mother worked to pay her school fees. Maybe it wasn't a purposeful choice to live simply.

Maybe they couldn't afford the stupid crap my parents love. Maybe Gin was right; we'd gone too far. Maybe we were beginning to ruin things. Lives.

TUESDAY EVENING

Gin's family room looked out on the greenway, complete with maintained walking path, just like our house did. I took the trail to Gin's, climbing over the chest-high fence and dropping into his backyard. I walked around a small vegetable garden, dead and empty at this time of year, on my way to the back door.

"You can always come to the front door. Ring the doorbell," Gin's dad said in his deep voice as he opened the door leading into the family room from the backyard.

As I shrugged, he added, "Or at least use the gate."

"I'll keep that in mind," I said.

Gin's father was dressed in athletic shorts and a muscle shirt. He sat down on the couch and resumed tying his basketball shoes.

The sound of nails on wood floors, combined with a periodic thumping noise of massive tail against hallway wall, heralded the arrival of perhaps the only one in the household I wanted to see other than Gin: Murphy, Gin's yellow Lab. His tail knocked a water bottle off the coffee table on his way to greet me. The bottle rolled under the couch and Gin's dad swore.

"Hey, buddy," I knelt down and ninety pounds of Lab body-checked me. I wrapped my arms around him, rubbing his chest, as his tail continued to whip back and forth so hard his entire butt wiggled.

"Harper, you want a Coke?" Gin's voice floated out from the kitchen.

"Yes," I called back as Murphy licked the side of my face. Gin showed up a few moments later with two bottles of Coca-Cola, the kind in real glass bottles and made with sugar.

Gin's mom is particular about that. No high-fructose corn syrup is allowed in the house. And she thinks frozen food from Whole Foods and Trader Joe's aren't "bad" dinners, although she has to be careful and make sure the meals don't contain dairy, or else she'll kill Gin. I knew he was going to offer me a frozen burrito or kung pao chicken within the next two minutes. Or maybe he'd offer me a smoothie with hemp powder. "I'll be back after my game," Gin's dad said, and he glanced at me and then back at his son. "Don't do anything stupid." Gin tilted his head and gave his father an exasperated look.

"We have more friends coming over soon."

"Don't worry," I added. "I'm not planning on getting pregnant. At least not until after prom."

"Your mom will be home from her book club...sometime." His voice trailed off as my words sunk in and he turned to me with wide eyes. I gave him my "I'm joking" smile. His eyes narrowed but then he gave me a rueful grin.

"My mom's at the book club too," I said. I didn't add that she'd complained this month's host always skimped and bought cheap wine, so it might be an early night. I offered to take the cheapo wine off her hands, and she didn't think it was funny. Gin's dad looked away from me.

"Finish your homework." He gave Gin a stern look.

Gin nodded as his father left. He waited until the door to the garage closed before he plopped down beside me and nuzzled his face into my neck.

"You know that look you gave your dad? After he told us to not be stupid?"

Gin sat back and looked at me with raised eyebrows. "You totally looked like your dad just then. Is that why he named you junior?"

"Maybe he just loves the name Gordon," Gin said before moving back to my neck.

"Gordon Isaak Nabb Jr.," I said as Gin pushed me down onto the couch cushions. "You're being a naughty boy with your hands."

"Will you shut up?" Gin's kissed me, and as I responded, he started to feel more intense, almost desperate, as he slipped his hand up under my shirt. His fingers spread across the bare skin of my belly.

I pulled away. "The others will be here soon." My voice was husky.

Gin's voice was even huskier. "They can wait."

I slid out from under Gin, who left his hand on my stomach.

"We should…you know… All of our friends are. Everyone else is. I want to. With you. Now. Anytime."

I smiled to myself when I realized Gin was too distracted to speak in full sentences.

"We will when the time is right," I said. I traced the pattern of the green-and-beige area rug in the middle of the room with my eyes while Gin fidgeted next to me.

"Ever thought about feeling ready soon?" he asked, but his voice was hopeful, versus pushy or angry or both. I wanted to reach for him, pull him back to me, feel him against me again. But even though I'd thought about it, and I mean it, something kept me back.

"Shouldn't we practice what we're going to say to Alex?" I asked.

"Just throw a cold glass of water on me next time instead of mentioning Alex," Gin muttered.

The doorbell rang, and we made eye contact. "That could be the devil himself," I said.

"Ha-ha." Gin adjusted his pants before going to answer the door, and I picked up my bottle of Coke. Murphy stuck his head in my lap with a hopeful look in his deep brown eyes. "Not you too," I said as he rested his head on my knee.

I rubbed behind his ears. "It's not that I don't want to, you know. I'm just not ready for anything other than scratching your head right now. Even if everyone I know wouldn't have a problem giving you a belly rub anywhere in town."

"S'up?" Benji and Paisley arrived in a cloud of strawberry-scented perfume that seemed to radiate from them both, although I doubted Benji dabbed it on himself. Paisley's dress made her look like an ice cream sundae with its flouncy red polka dots over a white underskirt, so I guess the smell made sense.

"Hey, guys," I said. Paisley came over to give me a hug and straighten my sweater. She gave me a wink as she pulled away. "No, it was totally JV," Alex said as he entered the room with Sarah, and his head was twisted to look over his shoulder. Gin followed along a few moments later with three bottles of Coke and a bottle of water.

Sarah took the water. "Coke has so many empty calories," she said. I raised an eyebrow at her. If she was doing her running and strength workouts for soccer, one soda shouldn't matter. She made a "what" gesture with her hands.

"But cola tastes so good," Benji said and gave an exaggerated sigh as he popped open his bottle and took a swig.

Sarah rolled her eyes as she sat down across from me. Gin slid between me and Paisley on the couch, while Alex took the solo La-Z-Boy chair as if it were a throne. Benji looked at the empty seat next to Sarah on the love seat and instead perched on the sofa arm next to Paisley. She promptly put her elbow on top of his leg and leaned against him. He gripped the back of the couch with his hand.

"So why are we meeting tonight?" Alex asked.

"We have something to talk about," Gin said. He glanced at me and then at Alex. "As a group."

And so it began.

ELEVEN

Gin looked around the room again before speaking. "We need to talk about the burglaries."

"Did Harper tell you about ours last weekend? It was brilliant," Alex said. "I wonder if we could get all of us together for once instead of just doing it in ones or twos. Maybe steal something big."

"I still can't believe you chose Harper instead of me for last Saturday," Sarah said.

Hmm, maybe Gin hadn't talked to everyone yet. Paisley's blue eyes were very round, which I assumed meant she was feeling serious, and her mouth was in a straight line, just like Benji's. Four is a majority, so maybe that was Gin's thought process. Or maybe he just didn't want to deal with Sarah when he didn't have to.

"We need to stop."

Everyone turned toward Gin. The smile slid off Alex's face. Sarah's eyes widened.

"Why? It's going great. I even know our next target," Alex said. "Guy in my weight training class is heading to Hawaii in a few weeks."

"This isn't a game anymore," Gin said. "It's getting too real. We could wreck our lives. I'm walking away, and I'm not alone."

"Really? Who else is chickening out with you?"

I recognized the sarcastic smile that took over Alex's face as he glanced around the room. It was the same look he gave the new kid who transferred in and said he would take over the starting point guard spot for sure since he'd started on a better team at his former school. It was the look that said Alex knew he was the chosen one. Even if he had to sabotage others to get his way.

"It's not just me. Benji, Paisley, and Harper agree with me." Gin's voice was steady. He maintained eye contact with Alex as if he was making sure Alex wasn't going to attack him. Like Alex was a rabid dog. Well, he's always a dog, I told myself.

"Et tu, Harper?" Alex said as he turned to look at me. His voice turned a bit flirty, and it felt like fingers scratching along my back. "Didn't we have fun last Saturday?"

I half smiled, even though I told myself I should remain as calm and focused as Gin. "It's over, buddy. It's not worth it." I rubbed behind Murphy's ears and he put his chin in my lap again, although his tail flicked like he was picking up the tension in the room.

"Chicken."

"Cocky bas—"

Sarah's voice cut me off. "Let's discuss this!" She sounded shrill. "I can't believe you've been talking about this behind my back."

"Why do you sound so panicked, basket case?" I asked, the words coming out before I realized I'd spoken out loud. "This isn't brain surgery."

"I'd rather finish my junior year having fun." Paisley's voice was high-pitched as she entered the conversation. She looked at the floor when everyone swiveled in her direction.

"Marisa Foret was devastated," I said. Her crying face from earlier crossed my mind with a wave of guilt.

"Who's that?" Alex asked.

"You're shitting me, right? Marisa Foret? We broke into her house last weekend. You stole her stupid Veg CD. What are you going to do with a CD? Do you even have a stereo that plays them?"

Alex's mouth quirked up in a self-satisfied smile. "What she'd say? You didn't do anything to give us away, did you?"

Marisa's red eyes and shaky posture crossed my mind again. "No, I didn't give anything away. But we shouldn't have done it. She didn't agree to it."

"That's not what you were saying Saturday night." He made it sound dirty, like we'd been doing more than just stealing worthless junk.

"Yeah, I loved running for my life when you broke that window on purpose." Afterward, it had been exhilarating, like I'd just finished a perfect five-mile run with rainbows lighting my way. But what if he'd done that to Gin? What if he'd made a wrong turn and was caught by the police? Or Paisley. She wasn't a fast runner and couldn't jump over a fence, even if the perfect vintage outfit was on the other side.

"We're out," Benji said, and my attention snapped back to the conversation.

"Yes," Paisley seconded. Benji smiled at Paisley, who gave him a nervous grin in return. She leaned against him even more, and his hand went to the back of her head.

Alex turned to stare at Benji.

"Seriously?" Alex asked, and Benji gave a small nod as he kept his eyes on his cousin, although he looked like he wanted to look away.

"Me and Harper are out too," Gin said. I nodded my solidarity with a straight face, letting the group know I couldn't be budged.

Everyone turned toward Sarah. She was playing with strands of her brown hair, pulling them apart and then twisting them together. Her brown eyes were staring at the floor.

"Thoughts, Sarah?" Alex said.

She shrugged. "If everyone is out, I guess I am too. Although I don't see why we're stopping. I'm sad I didn't get the chance for one more score, especially since Harper went last weekend. But if Benji and Paisley aren't brave enough to continue, I guess we're done."

"It's not a question of bravery," I said. I gave her a sarcastic smile.

"Whatever."

"We're keeping this quiet. No one talks," Gin said. He looked around the group, making eye contact with everyone. "This includes everything we did before, all of the break-ins, including last weekend."

"Yeah, yeah, it ends now," Alex said. "I get it, Mister Boy Scout."

Alex stood and held his hand out to Sarah. "Come on. Let's find some more exciting people to hang out with."

Sarah paused and looked at all of us in turn. Her lip curled as she looked at Benji and Paisley. "You should be grateful you get to hang out with us, and instead, you side with these nerds. Good thing I'm with the fun side of the family tree."

Sarah left with Alex, and the four of us remaining looked at each other.

"That went better than I thought it would. I thought Alex would make a bigger deal out of it," Gin said. He nudged me with his shoulder. I bumped him back.

"I thought he'd insult us more," Benji added.

Paisley looked at me. "Do you think Sarah's done with us? Will we still be friends?"

"You know what they say." I looked at Paisley. "If you love someone, set them free. If they don't come back, text them when you're drunk."

Paisley laughed, but it sounded half-hearted. Not her usual bubbly sounds. "Maybe this is the end," she said in a wistful voice. "All friendships end eventually, right?"

"They'll come around in a few days," Gin said. He sounded confident, although a thought took root in my mind. Did I care if they came back?

Maybe I should think of something nice to do for Marisa too. I didn't have any albums by the Veg, but maybe I could give her some songs I like on a flash drive. Something better than the craptastic tunes Alex had stolen. Something with a bit of soul and a side of angst. She'd like that.

TWELVE

WEDNESDAY MORNING: APRIL 13

Gin picked me up in his Jeep Wrangler before school, and we dropped Maggie off at the Richland School for the Deaf on our way. Gin turned up the volume and the bass on his stereo for my sister so she could feel the music pulsate through the seats. Gin signed, "Geocaching next weekend?" to Maggie as I waved goodbye to her. She signed yes to Gin and gave me a quick wave before disappearing into a mass of her classmates heading inside. She took a couple quick steps and caught up with a girl with a long braid down her back. Maggie had just left us, but she was already back in her own element. Her safe, supportive world.

"Have you heard from anyone?" I asked after Gin turned the music volume back down to a conversational level. I glanced down at my phone. My last text was a **What's up** to Paisley fifteen minutes ago, but I hadn't heard back. Hopefully, she wasn't still dwelling on whether Sarah hated her or not. The bazillion texts she'd already sent about it were obnoxious. "Benji texted before I left home and asked if we have a robotics club meeting at lunch."

"Exciting."

"I told him no, but I do have one for the Speech and Debate Team."

"I have other plans for lunch anyway," I said. "I'm meeting with the detention club."

"What'd you do this time?"

"Ms. Erickson doesn't have a sense of humor. She doesn't appreciate jokes about who in our class deserves scarlet letters."

Gin shook his head and then reached over and patted my knee. "That's my girl."

"You're lucky she doesn't teach the smart kids, so you don't have to deal with her."

"You should have taken AP English with me. You could have terrorized an entirely different group of people," Gin said.

"Eh, I've heard enough about that from my dad."

Gin suddenly slammed on the brakes and honked. A quick glance showed Gin's clenched jaw. He shifted gears like he was angry, jamming the stick into fourth gear as he sped on the highway, passing a car that was probably going under the speed limit. If it wasn't, Gin was definitely driving like he was auditioning for the Indianapolis 500.

My phone buzzed. Emma from my English class: *Is it true?*

What true?

You haven't heard? Must just be a rumor. Whatever.

I glanced again at Gin. I'd figure out a way to do something nice for Marisa, since anyone who lived in such a boring house and was in love with the Veg clearly needed a little something special in her life. Maybe I could convince Paisley we should take Marisa out for coffee. Although the thought of having to listen to her warble on and on about mundane nothings made me want to punch the Jeep's glove compartment harder than I'd punched Sarah just a few days ago. Was I really going to invite a wet dishrag like Marisa out for coffee?

The parking lot at school was almost full, and Gin pulled into a spot in the back. We grabbed our bags out of the far back of the Jeep, where they'd been wedged up against the door, and strode along in silence.

Gin put his arm around my shoulders as we approached the front door, making me feel like his security blanket. Or teddy bear.

"Doesn't everything just feel weird to you?" Gin leaned down and murmured into my ear.

I glanced around the front hall of the school. Usually there was a crowd of people hanging out by the inside benches, joking around. But there were only two girls there today, and they were hugging. But it was a desperate, clinging-to-each-other hug, not a "That A on the math test rocked!" or "Squee! I'm getting pizza on Saturday with Jimbo and all of his friends, but I know this means he thinks I'm his one and only. 'Cause I rock but I'm going to obsess over what I wear, and how I fix my hair, and every nuance of the situation from now until I get really old, like thirty."

Something happened and it had to be bigger than girl #1 on the bench's parents getting divorced, given the look of devastation on her face.

"Please go to your first classrooms." Principal Jeffries stood with his arms folded over his chest like a sentry overseeing the front hallway. No smile. Not even a small one.

"But the first bell hasn't rung," I said.

"No, it hasn't. But we're asking everyone to go to their classrooms as soon as they arrive. No lingering in the halls."

"What's wrong?"

"Go now, Ms. Jacobs and Mr. Nabb."

"What about those two?" I said pointing to the girls on the bench, but Gin was already pulling me away.

"Choose your battles." His voice was grim.

"I'm letting you pull me for the next thirty seconds."

Gin sighed and let go of me. "I know you're not fighting back. But whatever's going on, do you really think arguing is going to help? Especially for no reason?"

I straightened my dark red sweater. "You're right. But we haven't done anything wrong."

"Come on, let's head to web design. The sooner we find out what's going on, the better. I have a bad feeling about this." Gin led the way down the hall, and I followed.

"What's going on?" I asked the girl next to me as we sat down in web design, also known as the only class Gin and I took together this semester since he'd taken a math class at the community college over the summer and was now a level ahead. The corner of her mouth quirked up when she turned to me. "Someone claimed that one of our classmates OD'd or something."

"Weird." I glanced down to the pocket hiding my phone from the world. Paisley still hadn't responded. But Paisley was way too smart to do something stupid like overdose, so I was worrying over nothing. The heavy feeling in the air was just getting to me as everyone whispered among the rows of computers. I pulled my notebook and voice recorder from my backpack, feeling like I was the only person moving in the otherwise still room.

None of the computers were on, and as I reached forward to turn on the monitor, Ms. Gray spoke from her desk in the front of the room.

"Please leave the computers off, class."

"Why?" I asked.

"One, because I asked," Ms. Gray said. But her face softened into a half smile, telling me she wasn't angry with me. "Two, because we're not using them today."

"Why not?" Someone from behind me asked.

"I have an announcement, but I need to wait for everyone to get here."

Gin's hand snaked out and clasped mine. I glanced at him. Raised my eyebrows. He shrugged. "What could have happened?" he whispered.

I shrugged, feeling the sense of oddness that permeated the air. Everyone was tense, including Ms. Gray. And normally she was the most chilled out of any of my teachers. The one most likely to goof off with us. She loved to take a mean comment and spin it around on the sayer and make a joke. But when she did it, it didn't feel mean in return, just thought provoking. She'd made me laugh at my own stupid statements before.

I realized something. I liked Ms. Gray. One of the few teachers I actually wanted to see at school. If something was bothering her, it must be serious. All of my body felt tense, even my metallic-blue toenails.

Gin's thumb stroked a circle on the back of my hand, and I wanted to yank it from his grasp. His touch felt cloying. I wanted to feel free. To be ready to face whatever was coming with both hands ready to fight back.

But I let Gin hold my hand. He clearly needed some comfort. An anchor in chaos. And, for once, chaos that I hadn't orchestrated. A heavy feeling glued me into my seat, especially when Ms. Gray glanced my way again. She didn't have any of her usual sparkle.

A few more people trickled in before the bell rang. Ms. Gray stood up from her desk and walked around it to face us. Her face was all straight lines, thin mouth. Level eyes hidden behind clunky purple eyeglass frames.

"I have some sad news for all of you," she said, scanning the room with her eyes. "It's about one of your classmates. Please know that I'm here for you, as are the guidance counselors and other teachers. You're not alone."

Someone spoke up. I realized it was me. "What happened?" Gin squeezed my hand tighter, like he knew what was coming. Could it be Paisley? She was always glued to her phone.

"One of your classmates overdosed last night in her bedroom. It might have been suicide or just a tragic, tragic accident." My unanswered texts to Paisley flashed through my mind and I gripped Gin's hand as hard as he'd grabbed mine.

"Did she make it? Is she in the hospital?" I asked. Paisley's sea-blue eyes laughing at a joke flashed through my mind. Why would she harm herself? If I was going to describe anyone I knew as a ray of happiness, it'd be Paisley. She practically pooped sunshine and rainbows. She was too smart for a stupid accident; plus, we'd all been sober last night. No alcohol or pills in sight.

"Sadly, no. She was found too late." Ms. Gray leaned back against her desk.

"Who is it?" a male voice asked from the back of the room.

"Sarah Dietz," Ms. Gray said, and my gaze snapped up at her.

"Sarah? No way that bitch killed herself. She loves herself too much." My body froze when I realized I'd spoken out loud. "Sorry!" I added. But I knew the words were too late. Ms. Gray was staring at me, and she didn't twist my words around into a comeback that made me laugh at myself.

"Ms. Jacobs," she said. Ms. Jacobs. Not Harper. Shit, she was really mad. "Go to the office. Tell the principal what you said."

"Yes, ma'am." I threw in the title of respect as an apology.

I pulled my hand out of Gin's and picked up my bag.

"You don't always have to say what you think," Gin said.

"Didn't mean to," I said and walked out of the door with my head high. But the pit of my stomach wanted to puke.

THIRTEEN

WEDNESDAY MORNING, CONTINUED

"Ms. Jacobs. What a surprise to see you again." Mr. Jeffries, the principal, leaned back in his chair.

"You know you missed me." I plopped down in the visitor chair across from his desk. He still had a framed poster of a mountain with the word *achieve* printed beneath it on the wall above his bookcase. He hadn't changed his office decor since partway through my freshman year.

"Why are you here this time?"

"I spoke my mind without thinking about what I was saying. Ms. Gray took offense."

"How shocking that you put your foot in your mouth again. What'd you say this time?"

"I, umm, expressed doubt that Sarah Dietz killed herself, because she loved herself too much." The words sounded worse the second time I said them, even if I softened the statement. I leaned back in the hardwood office chair as if I was reclining in a comfortable spot. See? Nothing to be mad about.

Mr. Jeffries closed his eyes and turned his head toward the ceiling. He sighed, then lowered his head and looked me in the eyes.

"You played soccer with Sarah on the school team, right?" he asked.

I nodded. "Yeah, although she floated between JV and varsity last year."

"Your outburst in class was a little extreme, don't you think?"

"I could have phrased it better."

"Or not spoken at all," Mr. Jeffries said. He studied me for a second. "So tell me. Why do you think Sarah wouldn't have killed herself? You were friends, correct?"

Friends? Had I felt anything except animosity and disdain for Sarah for months? Although viewed from the outside, maybe people would think we are besties. My parents would answer yes. Gin might say yes. How was I supposed to define friends or friendship? I'd known Sarah most of my life. But watching her get mad had been as much fun as actually talking to her. I wondered how people at school knew about my hair-pulling fight in the mud with Sarah. Only a handful of my club teammates went to my high school.

A sliver of guilt worked its way from my mind down the back of my neck to settle deep inside myself. How had Sarah ended up overdosing? Had Alex and Sarah hoarded away something, and had she messed up? Was she trying to take the edge off of her anger from last night? But Sarah never did drugs on her own. It was more fun with other people. Taking selfies of one-person parties is ridiculous, and she wanted her life to be picture perfect.

"I just can't see her killing herself. She wasn't depressed or anything. She had a lot of plans. Goals." Like my starting spot on both our club and school teams.

Guess that was something I didn't need to worry about anymore. A pang of guilt chimed through my mind. Soccer shouldn't matter at a time like this.

"There's a grief counselor on-site today. You should talk with her."

"Nah, I'm okay."

"You can visit with her or get another day of in-school suspension. I'm sure you said something more outrageous than you told me. Maybe a profanity or two. Or ten given your history." A sad half smile spread across my face and I shrugged.

"Okay, I'll visit the grief counselor."

"Go now. I'll make sure she's expecting you."

Darn it. I hadn't specified when on purpose. I wanted to duck out of English since I knew we'd probably end up sitting in a circle, holding hands, and talking about our feelings.

"Okay."

Mr. Jeffries pulled a pad of hall passes out of his desk drawer and scrawled on one before handing it to me. "That will get you to the counselor, and she'll write one so you can return to class."

"Fantastic."

"And Harper?" His voice stopped me right before I walked out the door. "Not that I don't enjoy our talks, but I'd appreciate not seeing you for a while."

"Works for me, though you know these talks are the highlight of your week."

"So make it happen."

Of course Mr. Jeffries would want the last word.

Everyone in my next classes was quiet when I came in after talking with the grief counselor. The keyword for the day was subdued. People mumbled about overdosing, how much suicide sucked, and Sarah. Every teacher made a point of telling us about the resources available to us. If we took drugs, we could get clean. If we were feeling depressed, we had many resources if we weren't comfortable talking to our parents.

Finally, the bell rang for lunch. Paisley waited by my locker, her eyes as red and swollen as her nose.

"Harper!" She grabbed me around the neck and shoved her head into my shoulder. I patted her on the back. Guess I was more than just Gin's security blanket today.

Paisley stepped back. "How did this happen? Did you think she would…? She could…?" As her voice broke, she closed the distance between us and hugged me again.

"Hey." Gin joined us and Paisley hugged him too. I handed her a packet of tissues from my locker, which she tore into. Between Marisa and Paisley, I was going to need to replenish my stash.

"We need to get some information," I said. Gin and Paisley turned to look at me in unison.

"What?" Paisley asked. Comprehension crossed Gin's face, causing his eyebrows to pull in around his brown eyes.

"Details. The scoop. Information on what actually happened to Sarah. Did she OD? She knew her limits. She didn't do drugs alone." My voice was grim.

Gin's face reflected my emotions. "Agreed."

"I don't understand," Paisley said. Her eyes darted between us.

"Think about it." Gin's voice was soft, like he was trying not to upset her too much. "Honestly, do you think Sarah would have killed herself? Can you see her doing that? Do you think she was depressed?"

"She wasn't happy about what we decided last night," Paisley whispered in a hoarse voice. "She texted me that I was stupid and made the wrong choice. She said I was dead to her."

Gin flinched. "That sounds like Sarah."

"I hope my final words are more inspiring than Sarah's," I said.

"Harper." Gin sounded disappointed.

"Sorry, I just keep saying the wrong things today."

Paisley looked thoughtful. "How would we get information on how, you know, she did it?"

"Could you stop by and say hi to Sarah's mom? You know, like a condolence visit?" I asked. Gin turned to me.

"Great idea. Don't people usually bring food over when someone dies? Maybe we can pick up a pie from Whole Foods or something?"

"Blackberry is Sarah's favorite," Paisley said. Her face crumpled. "Was. It was her favorite."

"I'll text Benji and coordinate this. Paisley, maybe you can stop by Sarah's tonight," Gin said. "Where is Benji anyway?"

"Guys…" My voice trailed off. "What?"

"Do you think there will be a police investigation? Do they investigate suicides? Let alone ODs? Will they read Sarah's text to Paisley?" I said.

"Crap," Gin said.

"Find Benji. Let's figure out what we tell the police. What should we say we talked about last night? And one of us should talk to Alex. But don't text about this in case they look at our phones. Radio silence, guys. Word-of-mouth only and make sure no one overhears you."

"Honesty is the best policy," Paisley said.

"Yeah, but I don't want to go to jail for burglary if Sarah really did off herself or if it was an accident," I said. Did Sarah really overdose just to mess with us?

Nah, she wouldn't kill herself. No way. She'd find some other way to get revenge. Something she could do and then sit back and watch it unfold. Although she'd get anxious and overexcited and mess up the revenge before it had a chance to happen. Because that's Sarah. She was too angry last night to be depressed.

So what happened? She was careful not to take too many pills at once. She should have been smarter than to overdose. She wouldn't have taken any drugs alone. She was strictly a party-only user. She wouldn't have thought getting high alone would be fun.

Alex probably knows the answers. But the last thing I wanted to see was his smug, stupid face. Maybe Benji could question him. As cousins, of course they'd turn to each other in times of trouble. It'd be normal. Benji would stick up for Alex. Especially since his girlfriend died. So maybe we'll have to trick Alex to get the truth.

FOURTEEN

My English teacher was talking about the symbolism in the novel we were supposed to have read for class, although I hadn't bothered. I'd find a summary online before our test, or I'd get Paisley to talk about it. She liked to discuss the plot points and literary symbolism of the overly involved novels our teacher liked. If she chose something fun, like *The Sandman*, I'd actually read it. My thoughts slipped back to Sarah. I was still shocked we weren't talking about her in class, but our teacher said by this point in the day we probably needed a break and a chance to think about something else.

I wish I could think about something else.

The door opened and a freshman girl I knew by sight came in

with an orange slip in her hand. The teacher broke off lecturing to take it.

"Harper, you're wanted in the counseling center."

"Huh?" I sat up. Someone giggled behind me. Emma.

"You heard me. Get going so we can resume class."

I gathered up my notebook and yet-to-be opened novel about bell jars from the 1960s. I'd already been to the principal's office today and had a brief chat with the grief guru brought in to help us all get in touch with our feelings. Poor Sarah. All she'd ever wanted was to be Queen Bee, and now the school was doing all they could to keep the student body from following in Sarah's overdosed footsteps. So what could my guidance counselor want with me anyway?

If she wanted to talk about the impact of Sarah's death on me, I should start pulling out my hair and crying. Maybe that would get me sent home.

The freshman handed me the slip and then walked down the hallway, more slips in hand.

"Thanks for the talk," I called after her. She didn't look back. I stopped by my locker to shove my stuff inside and brush my hair. I'd left my yellow binder for math on top of my textbooks when I'd put things away before lunch, but it was standing upright. The wool beanie that had been on the top shelf of my locker was next to the binder.

Who'd been in my locker? More importantly, why? I frowned to myself as I slammed it shut. Someone was going to pay.

"Why are you in the hallway?"

An adult voice behind made my shoulders straighten. I pasted a bright smile on my face and held up my hall pass. "Just on my way to the career center."

As I walked down the hallway, the rearrangement of my locker gnawed at something deep inside of me. Gin had known all of my locker combos since the seventh grade, but he didn't have a reason to get into my locker. Would the police have searched it? The school?

Or someone else?

I pasted the smile back onto my face as I entered the counseling center, although the unsettled feeling inside me told me I should go someplace to think. Someplace quiet.

"Harper." The admin of the center stood when she saw me. "Right this way. Detective Parker is looking forward to talking with you."

"Detective?" So not the usual "How about you shape up, Harper?" talk with my guidance counselor. Pity, since it had been a few months since we'd recycled our talk of stale sentences that involved me not living up to my academic potential. I followed the admin to the empty office set up with a conference table. A man was seated, a pad of paper in front of him, although he was typing on a cell phone as we entered. "Harper Jacobs, this is Detective Parker," the admin said before leaving, shutting the door behind her with bang that caused the open blinds to clatter against the office windows.

"Sit down." The detective motioned to a seat across from him. He flashed me solemn smile, the kind that doesn't say "This is a joyful occasion" but it also doesn't say "The shit is hitting the fan and you're about to get a poop storm shower."

"How are you doing?" he asked as I pulled a chair out and sat down.

"Umm, fine."

"I heard you and Sarah Dietz were good friends."

He was still leaning back in his chair, like this was something chill. Not like he was asking me about my dead friend, who, depending upon who he talked to, was somewhere on the spectrum from best friend to bitter rival.

We could tap-dance around this all day, or I could just go for it. "Why would you think Sarah committed suicide?" I asked.

"I heard you expressed doubts about that," he said. "And I'm keeping an open mind since this could have been an accident."

Yeah, I'd expressed loud doubts to an entire classroom. Totally not surprised someone mentioned it to him. "There's no way she would actually do it. Not her style."

He leaned forward in his chair, his muscles relaxed, but his eyes were sharp as he stared at my face. "Did Sarah give you anything in the past few days?"

"Other than a headache?" I didn't mention the bruise on my ankle. Or the faded bite mark on my arm. Soon the only thing left of Sarah in my life would be a handful of photos tucked away in a box in my closet and some annoying memories.

"Any possessions? It's normal for suicide victims to give items they treasure away."

"Sort of the opposite of the Egyptians? Don't they pile things around them so they can take stuff with them to the afterlife?"

The detective turned his head to the side a few degrees while staring at me. "I guess that's one way to look at it."

I wished I knew how to blush on command. Or maybe I could just leave the room? It's not like I was in a police station, locked in a room with a mirror on the wall that was really a window so people could watch the interview without me knowing. Although who doesn't know that God-knows-who could be on the other side, so you need to be extremely careful about what you say? Seriously, who hasn't seen at least one episode of a cheesy cop show?

"Eh, what was that?" I asked, as Detective Parker said something.

"I asked about the altercation you had with Sarah in soccer practice a week or so ago."

"That was nothing," I said.

"I heard you had a 'rolling-on-the-ground-hair-pulling girl fight,' to quote one of your teammates."

Who'd ratted me out to the fuzz? So much for loyalty to the team.

"You look annoyed."

"Just surprised 'cause I thought the fight was over and done with. I'd forgotten about it."

"It happened less than a week ago." The detective's voice was dry. Was he hiding a sense of humor behind the badge? The expression on his face reminded me of the times I'd said something funny to Mr. Jeffries, but he knew he shouldn't laugh because I was in his office for causing trouble.

I shrugged. "Why worry about stuff that doesn't matter? Sarah was kicking me in a scrimmage, and I punched her when she called me a diva. But we hung out at her boyfriend's the next night. I doubt she offed herself because we rolled around in the mud. If anything, I bet the only people who still think about the fight is the boys' team, and that's just because they're sad they missed it."

I wished Gin was in the interview with me so I could have bet him a bottle of whiskey that the detective wanted to sigh or tell me to shape up. This was serious business. Instead, he stared at me.

The meaning of the situation settled down on me, pressing me into the chair. Sarah was gone. Forever. I should take this seriously and show it mattered to me that a girl my age—one of my friends— wasn't going to be around anymore.

"I don't want to sound mean," I said, the brash sound dropping from my voice. "Sarah and I are friends. It's complicated, but it's not like I'm celebrating. I still can't believe it happened. That she's actually dead. This feels like a big joke, except it's not funny."

"It's not a joke." His voice had moved into the sympathetic scale of voice tones. "I really would like some insight into your friend."

"What would you like to know?" So I answered his questions, and I mostly told the truth. Then he asked the question I'd feared most.

"I looked at Sarah's text messages," he said. "It sounds like she had a fight with a girl named Paisley. Do you know her?"

Something told me he already knew that we all hung out. "Paisley? Yeah, she's a good friend. But if she was having drama with Sarah, that was between them. I tried not to get involved when Sarah went off on people."

"Went off?"

"You know, tried to instigate sh—umm, stuff. But whatever it was, it would have blown over. Staying mad at Paisley is like getting angry at baby rabbits and sunny spring days. Just doesn't happen."

"Okay." He gave me that look again, like he was trying to decide if I was certifiable. I wondered how Sarah would have reacted to his questions, which caused a pang to shoot through me, punching me in the rib cage.

"Is there anything else? 'Cause I really should get back to class."

"Did Sarah do drugs?"

That should have been his first question, I realized. Not the suicide business. I shrugged my shoulders. "She wasn't reckless. I'm not saying she never indulged on the weekends, but she was in control. She was more focused on soccer and school and all that jazz. Nowhere near Junkie Land."

"How about you?"

I could feel my facial muscles tighten as I stared at him. "Never."

"Not even a joint? I'm not on the drugs squad. You can tell me the truth."

I shook my head. "Never. Nothing harder than alcohol. And I'm careful with that."

"So no trips to Junkie Land?" His voice was sarcastic. He leaned back in his chair again, lacing his hands behind his head and probably crossing one ankle over his knee under the table.

"It's not somewhere I'm ever going to visit."

"You know something about it?"

"Something like that."

He studied me for a moment before sliding a business card across the table. "Feel free to call me if you think of anything else. I'm sorry for your loss."

I stood, tucking the business card into my pocket. "Thanks." I paused by the door. "You should talk to Sarah's boyfriend."

"What's that?" his eyes snapped up at me.

"Sarah's boyfriend, Alex Conway. They were together all the time. If anyone had insight into Sarah, it'd be Alex."

"Thanks." He was still staring at me, so I left.

My steps were quick as I left the interview with the detective. Like I was running away from thinking about Sarah. About how she died.

About my responsibility in her death. Except—I wasn't responsible. I didn't kill her. I didn't want her dead. I repeated the mantra in my head. Even when I hated her, she was my friend. We'd been friends for a long time. Most of our lives. Maybe I even missed her a little. Or at least I would once she'd been gone for a while. After I'd had a chance to breathe. As I looked into the boring gray metal chasm of my locker, I told myself to cut the crap. Tell myself the truth.

I should have told the detective everything.

I should have told him Alex must have murdered Sarah, or at least given her the drugs she'd overdosed on. There was no other explanation that makes sense. He's a detective. Maybe he could find proof. Send Alex to jail.

My shoulders turned back to the counselor's office almost on their own. Like they were making the decision that scared me. I should go confess. After all, it's supposedly good for the soul. And maybe I can make sure Alex gets a longer prison sentence. He should since he had to be involved in Sarah's death. We broke into each other's houses, although with each other's permission, so it wasn't really that bad of a crime. But murder? Whole new ball game. Heaviness descended on the top of my head before dripping down like rain onto my shoulders. Bing-a-bang. Hands reached for my phone like a dog that's been trained to bark on command. I didn't recognize the user name—Penetr8er. But the number 8 is Alex's basketball jersey number.

Heard you talked with the police. How'd it go?

I glanced around the hallway, feeling like someone was watching me, before texting back. The halls felt deserted although I knew my friends and frenemies were behind the classroom doors. My phone dinged again.

Remember we're all in it together. We'll all go down. Keep your head in the game.

I know. I shoved my phone into my pocket and slammed my locker door shut. But my phone vibrated and dinged again. I pulled it out and unlocked the screen even though I knew I should ignore him.

There's one thing you should see.

My photo binged again with a photo. I opened it to find a photo of pill bottles. Prescribed to my mother. A row of blurry bottles was behind it.

So? I typed back. Like everyone's mom didn't have stuff like that in the house.

Think police would be interested knowing you have some heavy pharmaceutical crap? It's illegal to give drugs to your friends.

My heart beat in an angry staccato. As if I'd raid my mom's medicine cabinet to help Sarah get high the same night we'd argued. I never touched the drugs in the house. Ever.

I didn't give anything to Sarah.

That's not what the police will think if they find out she died from the same stuff.

A few seconds later, all of the messages deleted themselves from my phone like the app was programmed to do. My breath came in deep gasps like I'd been running.

"Ms. Jacobs?" a voice asked from behind me, causing me to jump. A voice I knew better than I should.

I held up the note excusing me for being late, turning it so it was visible to Principal Jeffries standing behind me. "Just on my way to class!"

"Texting in the hallway is not going to class. I'll excuse it this time if I see you hustle to where you should be."

"Just pretend I have wings on my sneakers."

I walked briskly down the hallway, not letting my footsteps slow until after I turned the corner. I suspected Mr. Jeffries was following me, so I knew I shouldn't pause before entering. But I still stood for a moment, listening to my heart still pound away in my chest.

"Save your drama for your llama," I muttered before straightening my shirt. Time for class. I pasted a half smile across my mouth before opening the door.

I'd worry about Alex later.

WEDNESDAY AFTERNOON, CONTINUED

My phone buzzed. *Meet at car?* Gin.

K.

Everyone in the hallway looked punch-drunk. The general aura of sadness hadn't lifted from the school. Not that everyone was showing signs of grief; two freshman boys were chuckling as I passed them to head to my locker for my final trip of the day to get my homework and jacket.

"Harper!" A girl from my English class, Emma, wanted to chat.

"I'm so sorry!" Someone from my web design class said. "Are you all right?" One of the sophomores from the JV soccer team looked like she wanted to hug me.

I gave small, sad smiles and quick nods of acknowledgment, but I didn't stop to talk to any of my classmates. But when I turned the corner, I slid to a stop.

Alex was leaning against the wall, talking to an auburn-haired sophomore from the girls' basketball team. She was tall with lean legs shown off in slim-fitting khakis that sang designer. Her cashmere sweater showed off a glimpse of her stomach when she reached up to brush hair back from Alex's face. She looked as if she was taking care of him, like he was fragile.

Her fingers moved to his face and she brushed a tear off his cheek. He wrapped his arms around her, she responded, and they pulled together in a close hug, her head against his shoulder.

I almost walked over to them and yelled, "Your girlfriend died less than a day ago and you're already hitting on chicks?"

"Harper!" Emma, whom I'd ignored a few minutes earlier, grabbed me in a hug. "I'm so sorry."

I patted her on the back. When I let her go, I realized Alex was gone.

FIFTEEN

"Caramel latte?" Gin asked me as we stood in line at the Strong Brew coffee shop.

I looked through the window of the main door, watching a yellow Volkswagen try to parallel park in front of the shop behind Gin's Jeep. Paisley ended up about four feet from the curb on her first attempt, and a black BMW honked loudly at her before pulling into the other lane, cutting off an SUV as it sped around her. The SUV honked as well, and Paisley's car jerked forward two inches before slamming to a hard stop.

"Harper." Gin nudged me with his hip.

"Yeah, I guess."

"Did you even hear what I asked?"

I smiled at him. "Sorry, I was watching Paisley try to park." We stepped up to the front of the line and Gin ordered an Americano and my usual latte. I turned back to see Paisley's yellow Bug finally come to a complete stop about four feet behind the Jeep and about a half a car length from the corner.

Benji's gangly legs emerged from the passenger side. Gin pulled lightly on my hand and I followed him.

"Why don't you sit down in the corner?" He nodded toward the far corner. "It's better than mocking Paisley's parking job."

"I wasn't mocking her. I'm worried about her."

Paisley and Benji entered the coffee shop, and she made a beeline for me. The whites of her eyes were still red, and they matched the skin on the bottom of her nose. She grabbed me in a hug. Again.

I patted her back. "C'mon, let's sit down." I led her to the table Gin had pointed out earlier. No one was seated near us, so no one would overhear what we talked about.

Gin joined us a minute later and handed me a latte in a ceramic mug. He sat down next to me, holding his coffee in both hands like he was cold. The bitter smell of his drink wafted over as I took a sip that was mainly milk foam and caramel.

Paisley glanced around the shop. "Is this where you brought me last summer?" she asked.

"Yeah, it is. Gin and I come here sometimes," I said gently. We'd come here for iced coffees last summer after walking through several vintage clothing stores. Paisley had bought a giant pile of dresses and convinced me to buy a brown plaid skirt and matching sweater that has sat at the back of my closet ever since. She'd said the mod look was made for me. Sarah had joined us after shopping for coffee, ordering a blended drink that was mainly sugar, cream, and ice with just a hint of coffee.

Sarah had hated coffee but forced it down with lots of sugar because everyone drank it. A fresh pang of sadness dinged me.

Tears gathered in Paisley's eyes. "Sarah said their blended mocha was really good."

Benji joined us, balancing two drinks and a plate with a peanut butter brownie and a dark brown cookie. "Want some?" he offered.

Gin shook his head. "Can't, but thanks."

"I'm not hungry." I said, and Benji shrugged at me before breaking off a large chunk of brownie.

"I'm starving, which makes me feel a little guilty," Benji said before shoving the chunk of brownie in his mouth. He struggled to chew it.

I stared at him and his eyes widened slightly as he swallowed. "Did you talk to Alex?" I asked.

He nodded. His voice was rough, almost choking from the brownie. "He said he didn't know what happened. He's devastated."

"Whatever." Him wrapped up in the arms of another girl didn't seem like devastation. Plus he knew what Sarah had overdosed on when he'd Snapped me.

Gin's arm nestled around my shoulders. His fingers tapped me on the shoulder; I turned and looked at him.

He leaned toward me and whispered "Chill" in my ear.

"Give me caffeine and then tell me to calm down," I whispered back. His snort sent a wave of Americano-scented breath across my face.

Gin's arm tightened and I turned to follow the path of his eyes. My spine straightened.

Alex.

SIXTEEN

WEDNESDAY AFTERNOON, CONTINUED

"Hey guys." Alex's eyes were rimmed with red, but his half smile was relaxed. His hair was artfully disheveled, like he'd been running his fingers through it all day. But it was arranged just enough to make me think he'd checked it in the rearview mirror of his car to make sure it was cool messy versus flat on one side and standing up straight on the other. Versus Paisley, who'd obviously been crying into her hands all day.

Alex pulled a chair over and turned it around so he straddled it at the other end of the table. He snagged the rest of the brownie.

"Benji was eating that," I said.

Alex turned toward me, but Benji spoke first. "It's not worth arguing over it, Harper. We have other things to worry about."

"I can always buy him another." Alex brushed a strand of brown hair away from his eyes.

"I can't believe she's gone." Paisley's voice wavered halfway through. Tears spilled down her cheeks, creating small rivers in the face powder she'd applied since her last cry.

My whole body tensed up. Gin squeezed my shoulder again. I took a deep breath, telling myself to calm down.

"I have to ask," Alex stared directly at Benji, "did Sarah raid the stash of drugs from the burglaries? You have the stash squirreled away with the money, right?"

Benji shook his head. "Whatever she overdosed on, she didn't get it from me. She could have snagged something from Gin's house when she broke in and kept it for herself. But I didn't see her go near the bottles of Valium and Ritalin I took to Alex's. She left early."

"Can someone even overdose on Ritalin?" Alex asked.

"If they took enough, yeah," Gin said. "Any drug can be toxic."

"Even vitamin C?" Paisley asked and we all swiveled to stare at her. Her mouth wobbled like she was about to start bawling again.

Gin smiled at her. "I assume so, but I'd have to research it to tell you how much would be fatal."

The whole table was silent for a moment. Benji stared at the table, his face blank. Paisley dabbed at her eyes with the napkin Gin had pushed across the table to her. Alex's foot tapped against one of the table legs.

I dropped a bomb into the middle of the table.

"No way Sarah committed suicide, and I can't see her overdosing. She wasn't that stupid."

Gin muttered my name and Alex snapped his head around to stare at me. "What are you suggesting?" Alex asked.

I glared back into his eyes. "That it wasn't an overdose or suicide."

Alex shook his head. "Who would want to *kill* Sarah?"

"You mean other than you? You had the best opportunity."

Everyone stared at me. Paisley's mouth was open. Gin rubbed his hand across his eyes. Alex clenched his hands and his entire face tightened. "How dare you say that."

"So you deny it."

"It must have been an accident." Benji's gaze darted between the two of us. "Harper's just upset."

"I can fight my own battles, Benji." Alex sounded dismissive, but there was a current of anger under his words. He didn't even look at his cousin and instead kept his eyes on me. Something about the look in his eyes told me he wasn't telling me everything.

"You're hiding something. And what was with the Snaps you sent me earlier, telling me to keep my head in the game?"

"What? I didn't send anything to you."

"Liar." I should have taken screenshots of everything.

Alex stood and leaned over the table. His hands closed in fists, and he put his weight on them as he stared at me. "I have no idea what you're talking about."

I stood and stared back. "Lying asshole."

"Harper, let's go." Gin stood, his body square to the table. Alex turned to look at him and they locked eyes. Gin maintained eye contact with Alex as he pushed me lightly toward the door, but I stared at the two of them. Gin was an inch or two shorter than Alex's six-two, but he's more muscular than Alex's lanky frame.

Benji jumped to his feet as if he'd be able to break up a fight between them. Gin put his hand on my shoulder and we walked out of the coffee shop, Alex staring at us the entire way. Paisley had her hands over her face, and Benji was focused on his cousin.

I took a deep breath when the door shut behind us. My hands trembled.

"I'm sort of pissed at you right now. That was mean. You can't go around accusing people of murder with no proof," Gin said. We walked up to his Jeep.

He turned and faced me. "And what about Snaps?"

"Alex sent them this afternoon. It had to be Alex. He asked what I told the police and warned me that I could get in trouble for giving Sarah drugs. But I didn't. Give Sarah drugs, I mean."

"I know you didn't," Gin said, and some of the anger pulsating through me simmered down, but I could still feel it gurgling inside me.

I looked Gin straight in the eyes. "Do you think Sarah committed suicide?"

He sighed and leaned against the car. "I can't see her doing that. But I also don't see Alex snapping and killing her. Why would he? It has to have been an accident."

"Snapping? Maybe he planned it."

Gin shook his head. "Not his style. He's not as bad as you, but he's reactionary. He's not a planner."

Reactionary? Like me? Was that true? Not that I hadn't been called impulsive before. Alex and I had planned the last burglary in advance, but it wasn't an in-depth plan. It was just chance that I'd known about Marisa's family being out of town. Would he have figured out a target and actually planned a break-in without my help?

Maybe Sarah's death was an accident.

Maybe I even owed Alex an apology. But something inside told me there was more to the story.

I looked up to meet Gin's eyes studying me. His shoulders weren't as tense as they had been, but he didn't look relaxed. Poor Gin. He'd gotten me out of the coffee shop before Alex and I completely blew up. He'd been willing to redirect Alex's anger toward himself. I sighed and stepped forward, reaching up to cup the back of Gin's head as I brought it down, so I could stretch up and reach it.

Gin pulled back after a moment. "Want to go back to my place?"

My phone buzzed in my pocket for the third time, and I held up one finger in a wait gesture before pulling the phone out and reading the screen. My father texting me to go home because he wanted to talk to me about what had happened today. I shook my head at Gin, although going home sounded terrible. "Another time."

A car started up behind us and I glanced back to see Paisley pulling away from the curb with Alex next to her and Benji sitting in the back. Alex glared at me as they drove past us.

Definitely not over.

SEVENTEEN

THREE AND A HALF YEARS AGO: OCTOBER

Everyone we passed laughed when they saw us, but Gin the Red-Nosed Reindeer pretended he didn't see them.

I adjusted the elastic holding the beard that completed my red Santa Claus suit and glanced at Maggie, who was trailing a step behind us. I felt like the fun-house mirror compared to their choices. Maggie's black-and-white striped shirt, black pants with suspenders, black beret, and white face paint, was monochromatic. Black tears on her cheeks completed her do-it-yourself mime costume. Only the orange plastic pumpkin in her hand added color to her outfit.

I signed at her. "You ready to call it a night?"

She nodded. I touched Gin on the arm, and he glanced at me. "Let's head back."

"Okay, but we have to hit up the house on the corner before we stop. They always give out full-sized candy bars. Maggie can't miss that."

I nodded and asked Maggie if she wanted one last stop, and she grinned.

"I'll do one more house for a full-sized candy bar," she signed back.

"Rock on," Gin signed back.

The house on the corner had a brick facade and fake skeletons hanging from the trees. Tombstones were lined up in the front yard. A figure came jumping out from behind the bushes after we passed them, causing me to jump slightly. But Maggie kept marching toward the front door.

"Tough little mime," the man who'd jumped out of the bushes said. The vampire fangs in his mouth caused him to lisp slightly.

I shrugged, and Maggie turned to see him. She glanced at me. "He tried to scare you."

Maggie smiled in response, but it was a sad smile, and she looked down. I put my hand on her shoulder and when she looked up, I let go and signed, "He thinks you're tough. You are too, tiger."

The man pulled a bucket of candy bars—Hershey bars with almonds this year—out from a potted plant on his porch. "You just need to say the magic words," he said.

"Trick or treat," Maggie said, the words coming out in her high-pitched voice, the words not quite formed the way they should be.

The man blinked slightly but then smiled, his fangs sticking out against the curve of his smile. He dropped two candy bars in Maggie's pumpkin.

"How about Santa and her reindeer?" he asked, and Gin and I held out our bags in unison. I wasn't asking for candy since we were chaperoning Maggie, but how could I say no?

"Thank you," I said as we walked away. We took the trail back to my house, bypassing the crowds of people out on the hunt for candy.

Gin paused under a light on the path and looked into Maggie's pumpkin. "Good job," he signed to her.

"Thanks," she signed back and was starting to say something else when there was another roar from behind us.

"Idiots," I said as Alex and Benji jumped out at us. "You two following us?"

"Three, actually," Benji said as Sarah followed along more slowly. She tossed her ponytail over her shoulder as if she was bored, and she had her arms crossed over her chest.

"Such a warm costume." I nodded at Sarah's genie costume that showed her entire stomach and most of her arms.

"Prettier than your stupid Santa suit," she muttered. She glanced at Gin and her eyes lit up. She dropped her arms down to her side and pushed out her chest. "Such a clever costume, Gin!"

Gin glanced over. "Umm, thanks."

"He's all about social commentary and comparing holidays," Benji said. He was dressed in black from head to toe, and I wondered if he was a shadow until I saw he was holding a marionette.

"Our costumes were Harper's idea," Gin said.

"Whatever." Alex looked bored in his fake-leather bomber jacket and slicked-back hair. His tone matched his expression.

Maggie tugged at my arm. "Guys, let's start walking again," I said. Maggie's face looked like every muscle was tight beneath the white face paint. Her I-want-to-go-home look.

My sister and I ended up a few feet ahead of the group, and then several yards, as we made our way home. Daniel was handing out candy this year.

"Wait up." Gin jogged a few steps and ended up by my side. Behind us, Sarah's shrill voice was saying something about us being too old to trick-or-treat.

"Alex, didn't you want to TP Silas's house over on Elm Street?" Benji asked.

"Yeah, we have to do that before we hit up the party at Paisley's!" Alex roared.

"Almost home," I said out loud while also signing to Maggie.

"You want to go for a walk after we drop Maggie off?" Gin asked. "Or we could head over to the party at Paisley's. Alex and the rest will head that way."

"Maybe."

Gin winked at me in response, and then he held the back gate open for Maggie and me so we could enter our backyard. "See you at the party!" Benji called as they passed by a few seconds later. He was trying to untangle the strings of his marionette as he trotted after his cousin.

"Wait, I thought Gin was coming with us—" Sarah's voice trailed off when Benji spoke.

"C'mon, Alex has a mission we need to help with."

"You okay, Maggie?"

"Just tired." Maggie's half smile made me wonder if something deeper was going on.

"I'm going to head over to Paisley's unless you need me."

"I'm fine." Maggie opened the door to the kitchen. "I'll tell Mom and Dad where you are if they ask."

Gin signed good night to Maggie, who nodded at him before disappearing into the kitchen.

"So, Paisley's?" Gin asked as we walked back toward the gate.

"Sure."

"We can take the long way if you're not sure about going to the party. But it sounds like fun. Even more epic than last year." I made sure the gate latched behind us, and after we'd walked about ten feet and were out of the glare of a light over the path, Gin stepped in front of me, stopping me. He looked me in the eyes. We were almost the same height, with me maybe being an inch taller at five-foot-five. But he'd almost caught up.

Unlike last school year, when he'd been two inches shorter than me during our class photos.

Gin took a deep breath and then leaned forward. Our noses bumped. "Sorry, I've never done this before," he muttered, and then our lips met. My heart fluttered in my chest. He pulled away from me and grabbed my hand. "On to Paisley's?" he asked.

"Maybe we can try this again," I said and leaned in. Our lips met.

He was smiling when I kissed him. After a moment, I started giggling.

"We'll have to practice," Gin said.

WEDNESDAY EVENING: APRIL 13, CONTINUED

Maggie was waiting by the front door for me when Gin dropped me off. "Is it true?" she signed.

"If you're asking about Sarah…yes." I didn't know how exactly to respond. Did Maggie think Sarah had committed suicide or overdosed? Or had my parents tried to keep the vulgar details from my little sister? Would the students at her school care that a slightly older girl had died, or would it seem remote to them? Like a death on a TV show, not quite real? As I studied the confused and sad look on her downcast face, I hoped they'd kept the details from Maggie. She's not even thirteen. Thirteen. Uh-oh. Maggie's birthday party was scheduled for this Friday. It would have to be canceled. Or would my father argue that life would need to go on? Would my mother be willing to have a party when one of the members of her book club was grieving? A headache started to pulse inside my skull. I wanted to leave, grab Maggie, tell Gin to pack a bag, pick us up, and drive away.

Maggie looked back up at me. "How are you? Gin? Paisley?"

"They're sad, but okay. Everyone's sad about this." A tiny part of my heart pinged when the impact of Maggie's questions settled in. She was more worried about my friends. About me. Maggie started to ask something, but her hands stilled as she looked behind me. Her face closed off as her emotions retreated back into herself. I knew that look.

"Where have you been? I texted you over twenty minutes ago."

My entire body tightened at the sound of the voice behind me.

"I headed home after getting your summons," I said. "I was out." I could see part of his reflection in the mirror next to the door. Rigid shoulders. No suit jacket, but he was still wearing a blue button-down shirt that matched the pinstripes of his trousers. I turned to face him.

"Your mother is over at Sarah's house," he said gruffly. He turned and we followed him back to the kitchen. He motioned to several containers of Chinese takeout from the local delivery place before disappearing into the garage.

Maggie looked at the food and then made a face at me but grabbed two plates from the cabinet and handed one to me.

Kung pao chicken, dumplings, and some noodle dish with bright orange sauce that neither of us touched.

"How was school?" I asked after we sat down. Maggie shrugged and bit into a dumpling.

The door to the garage opened and closed behind us, sending in a blast of cold air. Maggie shivered but soldiered on, clearing her plate of food. I took a few bites of chicken even though I wasn't really hungry.

Our father joined us a few minutes later, the container of noodles in his hand. No plate. He dug a fork in the noodles and Maggie wrinkled her nose at the sight of the orange sauce. Maggie had eventually decided she'd eat fresh oranges, but she still refused candy corn, pumpkin, and almost all other orange foods.

The silence felt heavy. Maggie stared at the table or her food. My father checked his phone between bites and fidgeted.

"Has anyone told Daniel?" I asked.

My father stilled. "Told Daniel what?"

"You know. About Sarah Effin Dietz. He knew her."

"I don't think your brother needs to hear about one of your friends overdosing while he's in rehab."

"It's not like he's never heard of an overdose before. Maybe he'll want to come to the funeral," I said. So the story being spread around was an accident versus suicide.

Maggie motioned to her empty plate. "I'm going upstairs."

"Okay."

"What did she say?" My father asked as Maggie stood.

"She's done."

Maggie rinsed her plate before putting it in the dishwasher and then ran upstairs.

"Good, I wanted a chance to talk to you privately."

Oh joy. I choked down one of the dumplings, which slid into my stomach and sat there like a brick.

My father put his phone down on the table and looked at me for the first time since sitting down. "So, Sarah."

"Yes, dead Sarah." He flinched, so I continued: "Who would have thought Sarah would be the one to die from drugs and not Daniel?"

"Harper, you're not funny."

"Who's laughing?" The anger I kept tamping down all day started bubbling to the surface as I glared at my dad.

He returned my glare with a gaze of steel. "Did Sarah get the drugs from you?"

"No!"

"I'm serious, Harper."

"I don't do drugs. I don't deal drugs. Do you really think I would after having a front-row view of what happened to Daniel? Seriously?"

"Stop shouting at me."

"Then stop patronizing me." I matched his intense tone although part of me wanted to protest. I hadn't yelled at him. I'd barely raised my voice. But if he wanted to hear what screaming sounded like, I could bring it. He had no idea.

He looked back down at his phone and swiped at the screen. "I needed to know if you were involved in any way. If you aren't, we don't have anything to worry about." He switched to a disinterested tone as he scanned his phone.

The words just slipped out when I realized I was no longer the biggest concern at this moment in his life: "I don't know if the detective that interviewed me today would agree." My icy tone matched his.

His eyes snapped back up to stare at me. "What detective?"

I shrugged, hiding a mocking smile inside. "The one who wanted to talk to me about Sarah. Wanted to know if she was depressed and would have committed suicide. Asked about drugs."

"What did you tell him?" All of his focus was bearing down on me. His phone was forgotten on the table even though it made a beeping noise and starting blinking.

"The truth."

"What did you tell him?"

I looked him straight in the eyes. "What I just told you. I don't do drugs. There's no way Sarah committed suicide."

A flicker of relief crossed his face before a stern mask covered it. "Next time a cop tries to question you, ask for a lawyer."

I smiled sweetly as I picked up my plate. "Why? What would I have to hide?"

EIGHTEEN

My tablet fit easily against my knee as I leaned back in bed. Deep breath, I told myself. Breathe deeply. Let it go. Ignore him. I was just waking the tablet up when my phone buzzed with a text from Paisley:

Did you see the tribute?

What? I typed back.

SchoolF.

I opened a web browser and navigated to the ridiculous school-run social media site, "SchoolFriends." I hadn't visited for months, probably not since we set up our profiles on the first day of school while being lectured about how this was the safest place for us to congregate online, since it was just registered students of the school.

Gin had mock-lectured me for weeks about using the school site when he saw me using non-school-approved apps. "Don't let me see you messaging with perverts and pedophiles, young lady," he said long after the joke had become boring.

My phone buzzed again, this time with a Snap of a red-eyed Paisley with her mouth open wide, as if she was in shock. I took a selfie with my left eyebrow quirked up and sent it before returning to the tablet. I logged in, getting the password right on the second try.

My notifications bar said 99+ messages, but my eyes quickly went to the center of the page and the words "Farewell, Sarah," complete with her yearbook photo. I knew everything about the picture. The emerald-green sweater she'd borrowed from me and hadn't returned for two months. The way her brown hair fell onto her left shoulder but was tucked out of sight on the right. We'd exchanged photos, along with Paisley, the day we picked them up from the school's photography service.

Sarah had loved her photo so much, I'd asked if she was going to tattoo it across her butt.

I clicked on the link to the tribute. Our classmates were posting photos; Paisley had uploaded one of the three of us from the fourth grade with the words "BFFs Forever." I sighed when I saw it; even if I hadn't seen her name attached, I would have known it was something Pais would write.

The yearbook teacher had posted a photo from soccer last fall. Sarah, me, and two of our teammates all grinned at the camera in muddy uniforms on a field with barely any grass left. Sarah had freaked out when she realized there was dirt smudged under her eye, almost like the sunblock football players use. "Own it, Sarah," I told her when we saw the photo. "Act like you meant it."

The back of my eyes felt scratchy as I clicked through the rest of the photos. Sarah in the stands at a basketball game cheering on Alex. She and Paisley drinking to-go cups of hot chocolate on the bench in front of the school. One from track our freshman year when Sarah had run the 400 meters for JV. She'd taken third in one of the combined meets with the varsity team, finishing behind two seniors. The coach tried to get her to try out her sophomore year, but she'd decided to focus on spring soccer. A candid from homecoming court, Sarah in a purple dress and me in red. We'd shopped for the dresses together to make sure we didn't match, although we'd bought identical black shoes with four-inch heels. We'd even worn the same size shoes. We'd practiced together to make sure we could walk without falling off the stage.

My phone buzzed, distracting me from the memories swirling around in my head, tickling the back of my eyes and making my throat feel tight.

What do you think?!? Paisley asked.

What did I think? My fingers paused as I debated what to tap back. *I can't believe Sarah isn't going to be in school tomorrow*, I finally responded.

My phone buzzed again. A Snap from Penetr8er. My shoulders stiffened. *Having fun Harper?*

What do you want from me? My fingers felt like they were on fire.

Just checking in. You were angry this afternoon, but you were also throwing up bricks.

Leave me alone, Alex.

My fingers felt so tense I wasn't even sure I could type, but I managed to take a screenshot before the messages vanished from my phone. I went back to the tribute but put the tablet down when I started to type sarcastic comments under every photo, although I didn't post any.

Buzz. Another text. But my breath escaped me in a whoosh.

Gin. *Talk now?*

Video chat? I replied.

OK.

I answered the video call from SuperGin. "You're not going to believe the conversation I just had with my parents," he said.

"Did they talk to you about the danger of drugs?"

Gin stopped and stared at me through the screen of the tablet. "Did your parents?"

I shook my head. "No, but my father wanted to know if I'd given Sarah the drugs she overdosed on."

Gin flinched. "Of course he'd ask that," Gin said. He rubbed the top of his head.

"Your mother was at home? My mom is over at Sarah's house."

"She came back while we were talking."

"So I received some more Snaps," I said. "I screenshot one of them."

"Forward it."

I picked up my phone from the bed and texted Gin the image. I could hear his ringer through the video chat, and his eyes left his laptop to look at his phone. His face hardened.

"I should go call him out on this. Why'd he lie about it this afternoon?"

"We need to be smart about this," I said. "Not impulsive."

Gin stared at me. "Please tell me you're not lecturing me about being in control."

"Something you said earlier made me think. We need a plan. You're right that we don't have proof of anything, and accusing Alex of murdering Sarah won't help since the only thing we can prove is the burglaries."

"So what do you want to do?"

I gave him a half smile. "I hoped you'd have some ideas. I'm reactive, remember? You're not."

"Let me think. For now, let's lay low. No one-on-ones with Alex or anyone else in the group until we figure out what his game is. Let's just get through the funeral."

FRIDAY EVENING: APRIL 15

"I'm sorry your birthday isn't very festive," I said to Maggie. She shrugged her shoulders at me in an exaggerated motion. Her face made a *whatever* expression that matched her shrug. The doorbell rang, the special light in the hallway flashing along with it so Maggie would know someone was outside.

I trailed Maggie as she went to the door from the family room, and a feeling of relief slid through me as I saw the figure standing as the door opened. Gin looked snazzy in a red shirt and dark jeans.

"Happy birthday!" Gin spoke and signed to Maggie. "The big thirteen!"

"Thank you," Maggie said out loud, but she was looking at Gin quizzically, and my first real smile for days spread across my face when I realized what she wanted.

Gin rubbed his jaw and then stopped so he could sign while speaking. "I think I forgot something."

"Whatever could it be?" I asked as I slid up beside him. Maggie looked at Gin, and then back at me, before returning to my boyfriend. Her green eyes were wide, and her eyebrows were starting to come together, her forehead wrinkling, as she stared at us.

"I think I have something in my pocket," Gin said and pulled a pink envelope out of the back pocket of his jeans.

I pulled a purple envelope out of the pocket of my hooded sweatshirt.

"I think these go together." Gin took the envelope from me and handed both to Maggie.

She tore into Gin's, ripping the back of the envelope, and pulled out a card. She ignored the image on front and instead read the slip of paper inside: a gift certificate for her and four of her friends to the escape room downtown. She tore into my envelope and scanned the gift certificate inside the card, this one to the gelato shop next door to the escape room so they could celebrate triumphing over the puzzles in sixty minutes, or brood over having failed and being kicked out after an hour. Although the time I'd gone with Maggie and one of her friends, she'd been focused and figured out the clues in forty minutes. She'd want to break that record with the new puzzle to solve.

"Now you can throw the sort of party you'd love," I signed to Maggie. Her eyes lit up and she threw her arms around me, then released me so she could jump up and grab Gin around the neck. He hugged her back before setting her down.

"I wondered why you wouldn't give me your gift earlier," Maggie signed.

"Do you want me to put those someplace safe?" I asked. Maggie nodded and handed the gift certificates to me, so I slipped them into one of the torn-up envelopes the best I could, glancing at the front of the card Gin had given Maggie. A red puzzle piece with the words "you're the best piece of the puzzle" was in a field of blue pieces. I smiled as I put the envelope in my pocket.

One of Maggie's friends waved to her, and they started talking, their hands moving quickly. Gin laughed. "I can't keep up with them."

"You sign well. You should take ASL again next year." I smiled at him as he put his arm around me. I leaned my head against his shoulder.

"Since you're being sweet, I should mention this is probably the nicest gift you've ever thought up."

"I wonder if you'll still think that when Maggie drags you to join her and her friends in an escape room. Phones and outside help aren't allowed."

"As long as you're there too." A small smile turned Gin's lips up, and he looked content. Not overly fake happy. The sort of happy you can't be, and absolutely can't show, two days after the death of one of your friends. An image of Sarah back when we were ten and swimming on a warm summer day crossed my mind, and I shoved it away. I was sick of being haunted by memories of her.

We walked down the hallway to the kitchen. A large chocolate cake with buttercream frosting with the number 13 was on the counter, and a large metal bucket of sodas was set up on a towel on the floor next to it. The kitchen table held bowls of chips, three different types of salsa, and a tray of goat cheese tarts. 'Cause no birthday party is complete without some sort of food in a mini pastry shell, even if Maggie's face wrinkled up in disgust when she saw them.

"Pizza will be here soon. I know Gin has to be hungry," my mother said when she saw us.

"Okay." I stared at my mother, but she just looked quizzically back. She still didn't remember that Gin was allergic to milk. I glanced back at the tarts. No one had touched them, although I could tell multiple pairs of thirteen-year-old hands had rummaged through the chips, leaving crumbs behind on the table and streaks of salsa.

"I'll figure out some food for us," I told Gin. "The salsa should be safe for you, and there should be extra in the fridge."

"I had dinner already."

Gin and I grabbed two of the kitchen chairs and sat on the edge of the family room, watching Maggie and her friends sign away. Two of them glanced back at us and back to the rest of the group of six girls.

One of Maggie's friends broke away from the pack and walked in our direction. She signed hi to us but was looking at Gin.

Gin signed back "How are you?" and her entire face turned scarlet. She turned back around and rejoined the other girls.

I elbowed Gin. "You have an admirer," I laughed.

"Are any of Maggie's soccer teammates coming?" Gin asked.

"Not today. This is just friends from school. She's having pizza and cupcakes with her teammates after practice one day next week to celebrate her birthday since the big party was canceled."

"Poor Maggie."

"It would have been a weird mix. This might actually be better. Two different parties for two different worlds." Part of me wanted my sister to have a giant, mega, blowout of a party. Make her soccer friends meet her school friends. Maybe next year.

From the corner of my eye, I saw my father walking down the hallway from the front door. But that's not what made me stop and stare.

Daniel was with him, dressed in a gray sweater and tan corduroy pants. His hair was shiny and flopped over into one eye. He flashed me a grin, probably enjoying that I was sitting there with my mouth open, staring at him.

"Hey, buddy," Gin stood and shook Daniel's hand. My father ignored us and headed toward the goat cheese tarts.

"Hey." Daniel glanced at Maggie's group of friends before looking back at me. "I'm just home for the evening."

"Maggie will—" my voice trailed off when Maggie jumped across the room to give Daniel a flying hug.

"Happy birthday," Daniel signed at her once she let go. She beamed at him.

"Come meet my friends." She grabbed Daniel's hand and led him away from me.

"He looks good," Gin said.

"Better than he has for a long time," I whispered back. Daniel reminded me of his old self, the boy my friends had fallen in love with when we were freshmen. Would he make it this time? If I could have crossed my fingers, clicked my heels, done something to make sure Daniel would stay clean, I would have.

NINETEEN

Everyone was dressed in black. Including me in a knee-length cotton dress, black tights, and black ankle boots. All covered by my black peacoat. The same jacket I used when I broke into Marisa Foret's house and Sarah's home. Plus there was a black headband perched on top of my head like a gothic cherry on top of a sundae.

Beside me, Maggie stood with her head bowed. She'd kept her hands crossed in front of her during the service, and now she stood with them at her side. She seemed so calm, still; what was going on inside there? For all I knew, she'd spent the service reciting the multiplication tables.

Gin was on my other side, and Benji and Paisley were standing across from us. Benji's arm was around Paisley's shoulder, whose face was covered by the wide brim of her vintage black hat. From the way her shoulders shook, I knew she was crying. Between us was a shiny brown coffin above a grave in the cold spring ground. Who designed the contraption that holds the coffin up before slowly lowering it down into the earth?

What had people done before, just dropped the coffin into the hole? I flinched and told myself to shut up.

"She was too young," someone said behind me, echoing a sentiment I'd heard mumbled repeatedly all day. I wanted to scoff at all of them. Snarl. She was old enough, old enough to drive. Old enough to break into Gin's house and steal his mother's diamond watch.

Old enough to fall in love with the wrong boy. The absolutely wrong boy, as it turned out.

My parents were murmuring behind us. I put my arm around Maggie, and Gin put his arm around me, in a sort of three-person domino effect.

A figure caught my eye. Dressed in a dark suit, with navy tie, Alex stood at the back of the gathering. He stepped backward, moving away from the crowd of people. When we made eye contact, he winked at me and continued retreating from the burial.

I looked away, but my eyes were drawn back to Alex. But he was gone.

Sarah's house smelled like food. My mother carried a glass casserole dish of macaroni and cheese with mixed vegetables. It looked homemade, but really she'd bought food from the hot bar at Whole Foods and dumped it into a dish from our kitchen. Luckily, I'd been there to remind her to wash the dust out of the pan first.

"Thanks for coming." Sarah's mother hugged all of us. Her red-rimmed eyes were a contrast to her perfectly coiffed brown hair. Sarah would have looked exactly like her mother one day. Same long legs. Same slender hands.

"We're so sorry…" I walked into the kitchen. Several rotisserie chickens sat on the counter, along with three potato casseroles, a plethora of salads, and mounds of desserts. I snagged a chocolate chip cookie, wondering if chocolate can really cure everything.

Or maybe that's wine. My mother already had a glass in her hand, which my father tried to take, but she weaved her way around a few people, leaving him behind. There were familiar faces from school and soccer in the house but none of my friends.

"It's so sad about Sarah," a woman said behind me. "She was going through a challenging time, and even at sixteen things can look bleak, but who knows what sort of woman she would have turned into?"

I rolled my eyes and stepped over to the sliding glass door. I recognized the figure with brown hair standing on the patio, just beyond the covered area from the deck above. James. Sarah's older brother. Maybe twenty years old since he was a grade or two ahead of Daniel.

"Want some company?" I slid the door shut behind me.

"Sure." He didn't even look back to see who was joining him.

"I'm sorry for your loss." The words came automatically to my lips. It's not like James hadn't heard this already today at least fifty times. Maybe more. I stepped into the sunshine, although it wasn't any warmer here than it had been at the funeral.

He turned his head and looked at me. Brown eyes like Sarah's. He'd been a senior my freshman year, and I remembered hearing him give a speech as student body president. Not that I'd paid attention to anything he'd said. But I remembered him standing behind the microphone, some of the girls on my class listening intently to every word. He'd looked happy. Confident.

Now he looked like he'd been run over by my dad's Range Rover.

"You and Sarah always had a love-hate relationship," James said.

"I'm sorry for your loss," I said again. Idiot. There had to be something I could say. Do. Maybe say something nice about Sarah? Mention the time she waited for a tow truck with me after practice when I had a flat tire even though she could have driven herself home? Talk about how happy she'd been last fall when she'd been chosen as one of the students of the month at school? How she'd been so proud to start the final two soccer games, even if it had been at left fullback instead of midfield like she preferred? How much fun we'd had when her dad signed us up for the gun-safety class a year ago? We'd thought the class was boring, but then we had fun pretending we were Charlie's Angels. But safely, of course. After the first warning. Our instructor almost had an aneurysm when Sarah held a gun out to the side, in the direction of a classmate, with her hip out in official Angel style, especially since the gun had been loaded.

We stood in silence for a moment as I debated which Sarah factoid to offer up along with the casserole of mac and cheese we'd brought.

"So, are you going back to Northwestern soon?" I finally asked. "Or are you sticking around for a while?"

"I'm here this weekend, but Mom and Dad want me to go back to school ASAP. They think it'd be good for me to have something to focus on instead of dwelling on Sarah. As if I can concentrate on anything else." Bitterness colored all of his words. "Harper, you were Sarah's best friend. Was she using often? You know the signs."

The words "not my best friend" halted on my tongue. I swallowed, words swirling through me but none popping out. How would correcting James help? "She wasn't abusing drugs, not as far as I could tell. I'm not saying she never indulged, but it was just an occasional weekend thing."

"Like me," James said. "Although I'm never touching them again."

"A lot of people use without OD'ing." The words sounded absurd to me, and I glanced at James to see how he'd react to something so dumb.

"Do you think she meant to?" He sounded as if this was the question he really wanted to ask. He looked at me. I stared straight back.

"No." I didn't even have to think about the question. "No way."

The door slid open and then shut behind us. I didn't turn to look behind us; I kept my eyes on James. The grief in the brown eyes that stared at me, searching for answers I couldn't give. I wished I could. "I wish I could help," I whispered.

"Here you are," Gin said as he stopped beside me, glass of something in his hand. I grabbed it from him and took a sip. Iced tea.

"Sure, you can have some," Gin said as I handed it back.

James sat down on a wrought iron chair in the shade of the deck and leaned over, propping up his head with his hands. None of the chairs had cushions. I wondered if Sarah's parents would bother uncovering the barbecue set when the weather warmed up, or if it would stay this way all summer. Prepared for cold, for winter. Even if it was warm, would summer ever come again for them?

"Hey, everyone." I spun around at the sound of that cocky voice. How dare he talk to me?

"Hi, *Alex*," I spit out. He'd entered the backyard through the side gate, skipping the inside of the house.

He raised an eyebrow at me. "Be civil, Harper," he said, the tone of his voice mild. Like we'd just had a minor argument. Versus me knowing he'd killed his girlfriend. I just didn't know if he'd done it on purpose.

Gin put his hand on the small of my back. "Didn't know you were here."

"I had an errand to run, so I'm a little late." Alex turned to face James. "I'm so sorry. I wish I had known so I could have done something."

James stood, his face tight. His mouth was drawn in a straight line. "Shove it, Alex. You can't tell me there weren't signs she was going to commit suicide. And if she didn't, you must have provided the drugs. That's always been your thing. Like when you were a punk freshman trying to making friends with popular kids."

"I was always a popular kid." Alex sounded amused.

James turned and stormed inside. I glanced up at Gin, who was staring in James's direction, and then looked back at Alex. Alex was smiling like this was a happy occasion. I wanted to say "smug bastard," but the door slid open again.

"Gordon, can you come in here for a moment?" Gin's mom asked.

I turned to him. "I'll come with you—"

"Harper, I need to talk to Gordon alone for a sec. He'll be back in a minute."

Gin squeezed my hand and glanced toward Alex. "I'll be back soon or wait a few seconds and follow me inside," he whispered in my ear before patting my back one last time and stepping away. His mother shut the door behind him.

Alex smirked at me. "Afraid to talk to me without your boyfriend around? Thought we were friends."

"Yeah, well, I know what you did. You really think I want to be friends with you now?"

He stepped closer to me, and I stood my ground. If my eyes had been lasers, they'd have burned holes through him. He stopped about two feet away. My hands closed into fists. "You know that we should be more than friends," Alex said.

I snorted. "Whatever."

"Sarah was just a pale version of you. An imitation," Alex said. "I'm sad she's gone, but you're the prize I want. Her death clears the way."

He inched closer. I felt like spiders were crawling over my skin.

"Back up. Now. I'm not interested, Alex."

"Yes, you are." His smile was sly, as if he knew something I didn't. "Look for my present."

"Your present—?"

The swish of the sliding door opening caused me to trail off. "Harper, we're going."

Saved by my dad. I looked back at Alex.

"This isn't over." My voice was quiet enough so it wouldn't carry over to the door, but it still radiated authority.

"It's just beginning." Alex's voice was equally quiet and confident.

I backed up a few steps and then turned my back on Alex. My father had already retreated inside, and I locked the door when I went inside, leaving Alex outside.

TWENTY

"Why's the front door open?" my mother asked as we pulled into the driveway after leaving Sarah's house. I glanced at the clock built into the dashboard; we'd barely spent any time at the wake. The front of the car smelled like wine.

I glanced over at Maggie who signed, "What?" to me.

"Front door is open," I signed back. Her eyebrows crinkled as she sat upright to look at the front of the house.

"Who forgot to shut the door?" my father asked as he pulled the Range Rover into the driveway.

"Is Daniel out of rehab?" I asked. We'd left through the garage door, so we hadn't used the front door. Had we?

No one answered and I didn't bother translating for Maggie. "What if there's someone inside?" my mother whispered, as if the mythical person inside would hear her if she spoke in a normal voice.

Dad sighed. "I'll check this out," he said and climbed out of the car.

"I'll help," I said as my mother said we should call the police.

"No, Harper, stay here with me!" My mother's voice was sharp, a bit panicked. She turned and signed at Maggie, her hands forming sloppy signs.

Dad went around to the side door of the garage, leaving us to sit in silence. A few minutes later he came out the front door, golf driver in hand. He motioned for us to come.

"Was there anyone inside?" Mom asked, her words slurring.

I glanced at her; how much had she had to drink?

"No. But I'm calling the police." He turned and marched toward the front door. We followed, Maggie patting my arm and signing "What?" at me.

"Why call the police?" Mom asked. Did she have a flask hidden in her purse or something? I sniffed the air to see if there was more than wine circling the air around my mom, but I didn't get a whiff of anything else.

"Because someone broke in," Dad said. "Harper, Maggie, stay in the front yard. Don't mess up any evidence."

I put my arm on Maggie's shoulder and she looked at me. "Come with me," I signed and walked back to the Range Rover. I explained and then pulled my cell phone out of my pocket.

I texted Gin. *Someone burglarized my house.*

He replied instantly. *What? Do you need me?*

Dunno.

There in a minute. You need anything?

I glanced at Maggie, who was shivering in her thin black jacket and cotton dress. My black boots and wool jacket were warmer. I unwound my scarf and put it around Maggie's neck before texting Gin back. *Hot chocolate for Maggie. She's cold and we're supposed to stay outside.*

Gotcha. See you in a few.

I tried the door to the car, which was locked.

"I'll get the keys so you can wait inside," I talked and signed to Maggie.

"It's okay."

Mom and Dad walked out of the house. My father still held the golf club. What would he have done if there really had been an intruder? Putted him across the room?

His face was drawn, tight. Like the time the hospital had called because Daniel was found OD'ing in the bathroom of a club downtown. Mom held his arm on the side that was not holding an implement of golf destruction.

A police cruiser showed up seconds later, its lights on but without a siren. A face peeked out of the window across the street in a swish of curtains.

Dad was on the police officer as soon as he stepped out of his car. "What's going on in the neighborhood these days?" he ranted. "What's the use of having a security system if the burglars are smart enough to bypass it?"

"I'm sorry, sir. How about you tell me what happened? We can figure out what happened with your security system later."

"This area is going downhill," Mom slurred as she joined us and leaned against the car.

I wondered how she'd react if I told her the crime spree was partially my fault. Although. Motherfucker. I stood upright.

Alex did this.

Did he still have the alarm codes for our houses? I'd gotten my key back, but had Alex made a copy? This must have been his "errand" and why he arrived late to the wake.

I wanted to pace but my mother and Maggie were staring at me. I leaned back against the SUV, ignoring the looks my sister gave me.

Was this Alex's present? Chaos?

Another car pulled up and Detective Parker emerged. What was Detective Parker doing here? Didn't his business card say he was a homicide cop?

"Hi, Harper."

I felt my checks flush as he used my name. "Hi, Detective."

"How do you know my daughter?" my father demanded from across the driveway. The patrolman must have gone inside the house.

"I met your daughter while investigating the death of one of her classmates." Detective Parker sounded smooth, and he offered his card to my father. "I was in the area when the call went out over the police radio so I stopped by." They walked to the front door of the house.

Gin pulled up behind the detective's car. He hopped out, walked around his car, and then disappeared behind the open passenger-side door of his Jeep and emerged with a tray of drinks from the neighborhood coffee shop. He had a blanket folded over one arm.

"Hi. Mrs. Jacobs, Maggie," Gin nodded at my sister and then put the drinks down on the hood of the SUV. He then signed and spoke. "Harper told me what happened, so I brought some coffee and a hot chocolate for Maggie."

He pulled the cocoa out of the drink carrier and handed it to Maggie, whose face lit up. She held the drink close before taking her first sip. He put the blanket over her shoulders like a shawl.

"Sugar-free vanilla soy latte for you, Mrs. Jacob." Gin handed my mother her usual drink. How had he remembered?

"You're so thoughtful," she said as she took the drink from his hands.

"Caramel latte for you," he handed me a drink and then took the fourth for himself. I glanced at the loopy writing on his cup. Americano for Jim. I smothered a smile.

The supersweet flavor of caramel and whipped cream coated my tongue as I took a sip. I wished my mom and Maggie were far away so I could talk to Gin. How could I get them to leave? Or was there a way I could go somewhere with Gin? Gin leaned into me ever so slightly, his shoulder barely touching mine. He felt warm, like a solid rock of stability.

Maggie nestled into his other side, and he put his arm around her.

My phone buzzed, and I pulled it out of my jacket pocket.

It was Paisley. *You at the wake? I don't see you.*

We left early. Talk later.

Check SchoolF. Later.

My drink was cold by the time I sucked down the pure caramel that had nestled at the bottom. The detective appeared at the front door.

"Can you all come in, please?" he asked. "We need to figure what was stolen."

"Why do the girls need to do this?" my mom asked.

"Because they need to inspect their bedrooms."

TWENTY-ONE

SATURDAY AFTERNOON, CONTINUED

My heart thumped when I stepped inside my room. My red comforter had been torn off the bed and the mattress upended. My dresser drawers were dumped in the middle of the room, along with the contents of my desk and nightstand. My favorite photo—one of me standing with Paisley, Benji, and Gin at the Winter Formal last year—was on the floor of the doorway, and the glass covering the frame was broken like it had been stomped on. A photo of Sarah, Paisley, and me during the gun-safety course was torn into pieces and sprinkled on top.

But that wasn't what made me stop and stand still. I wanted to turn around and run and find Alex and beat his head in.

"Can you tell if anything was stolen?" Detective Parker asked from behind me.

"I think my laptop is missing. It was on the desk when I left. I'm going to need to go through everything before I can say if anything else is gone," I said. I worked my way around a mound of lingerie, which was next to a pile of books. The covers were torn off. I picked up the book on the top of the pile, which had been torn in half, with the remnants of the cover stacked on top. *The Last Unicorn* by Peter S. Beagle. My grandmother had given it to me, and we read it together the summer before she died of cancer.

Alex was going to pay for this. Slowly. Painfully.

"The rest of the house isn't as ransacked as your room. Any ideas why?"

I didn't look at the detective as I shook my head.

"No drugs?" His voice was quiet, like he didn't want anyone to overhear. Should I encourage him to go in that direction? Let him think I was into all sorts of nasty stuff. After all, my brother had been on his way to being hooked on cocaine at my age.

I turned around and looked him in the eyes. "Like I told you before, I don't do drugs," I said. "We're tested for sports at school. Feel free to check." My eyes strayed over to the pile of soccer trophies by my desk. Broken soccer figures from the trophies littered the floor.

"You sure you don't know anything about this?"

Cool gray eyes appraised me, and I studied him in return. He was hesitant to believe me. But why should he trust me? In the same situation, would I trust myself? It's not like I was trustworthy. I did know what had happened. But if I told, I'd get more than Alex in trouble. I'd take poor Paisley as well as Gin and Benji down with me.

"Maybe it was some freak who gets off on teen girls' bedrooms. Maybe he thought he'd find the good stuff in here. But if you're wondering about drug connections, check out my mother's bathroom. The medicine cabinet is locked, and that's where she keeps her Valium. There and in her purse. Her doctor prescribes it."

"You just go right for the jugular, don't you?" He sounded slightly amused, like I was a puppy trying to do a big dog trick.

"People always skirt around serious issues. Why bother?" I turned away from him and viewed the pile of destroyed birthday cards from friends and ripped-up homework in yet another pile, which I stepped over to peer into my closet. Everything was off the hangers, and something had been poured over the whole mess of fabric. I leaned down and sniffed. Beer? Probably the Belgian stuff my dad keeps in the fridge in the garage. But the scent of beer wasn't my biggest problem. This was my brother Daniel all over again. Multiple versions of what could be the truth were popping up, and I couldn't push everyone toward the right one. I felt powerless. My pulse felt like I'd just sprinted down the length of the soccer field. We'd agreed: we wouldn't steal from each other.

But it's not like Alex had been playing by the rules for days now.

So why should I?

Alex's words echoed through my mind. *Hope you like my present.* I glanced around the destruction of my room. Was this the present? Or had Alex hidden something among the piles? Like a grenade.

"You look thoughtful." The detective's words invaded my thoughts. He was still observing me like I was a rat in an experiment.

"What's that supposed to mean? Should I look excited someone trashed my room? I'm just debating how to clean this up." Maybe I should just confess. Tell the detective everything. A deep voice spoke from the doorway, causing my confession to jump back deep inside me before it had a chance to escape. Detective Parker kept his eyes on me, like he knew I had been about to say something interesting, as he asked the patrolman if it could wait.

"No, the homeowner is quite insistent he talk with you right now. Something about a missing passport."

"I'll be there in a moment." The detective still stared at me. "Was there something you were going to say?"

I shrugged. "If you talk to my sister, make sure you talk slowly and look at her. She reads lips well, but she misses stuff."

"Anything else?"

"No."

He looked at me one last time before he left, like he knew there was something I wasn't saying.

I shut the door behind him, debating how to go about tackling the mess. I pulled my phone out of my pocket and texted Paisley that we needed to meet soon.

I could start with the clothes in the closet. All of that needed to be washed, as did my lingerie, unless I wanted to go to school smelling like a brewery. My stomach roiled when I thought of Alex pawing his way through my personal items. As I turned, my jacket caught my eye.

It hung on the back of my door in its usual spot. Maybe Alex hadn't noticed it since it was out of sight when the door was swung open. Something about it, so untouched, drew me to it. I touched the dark brown faux-leather fabric, remembering how Maggie had insisted I buy a vegan jacket. The left pocket was empty.

As was the right.

But there was something sticking out of the small pocket on the chest. A pocket I never used.

Whatever was in the pocket was small. Square. Part of me debated calling Gin and asking him to come back, that I didn't care that my father had asked him to leave so we could go through the house in private. If I said I needed him, Gin would come over despite my father's nasty looks.

I took a deep breath, squared my shoulders, and unzipped the small pocket. I slid my fingers inside.

I pulled out a small packet wrapped in white notebook paper. On the outside of the paper was a loopy heart that didn't look like something Alex would draw. It was rather girly, from the shape of the heart to the pink ink. Like the sort of thing a silly girl would draw for her boyfriend.

Weird. I shook my head and unwrapped the paper, and a small chain fell out into my hands. Along with an unopened condom.

"Jerk!" I tossed the condom away from me. It bounced off the door before falling to my feet.

I ran the length of the chain through my fingers until I came to the charm. Really, it was three charms. A tiny drawing of a plum blossom in a silver frame, a purple glass bead, and the letter S.

TWENTY-TWO

SATURDAY AFTERNOON, CONTINUED

I knew this necklace. Alex had given it to Sarah for Christmas. She'd worn it almost every day since then. Even if it clashed with her outfit. My breath left my chest with a whoosh. What was I supposed to do with this?

A knock on the door made bubbles of panic erupt in me. I scooped the condom up off the floor and shoved it, along with the necklace and drawing of the heart, into my pocket.

I opened the door. Maggie stood there, and she was scrunching her hair in one hand.

"What's wrong?" I asked and signed.

"My journal is gone."

"What?"

"I went through my room. My journal is gone. Along with my favorite necklace."

"I'm sorry." I turned my head toward my jewelry box, which was smashed on the floor. Alex had left me a necklace, but had he taken one in exchange?

Maggie patted my arm, and I turned back to her. "Why would someone steal my journal? It's personal. It's not worth anything."

I sighed as I studied her face. "I don't know."

The lie tasted bitter, but the truth was too much to tell my little sister. That someone like Alex would enjoy reading her private thoughts. Most people offer to help someone if she's sitting on the ground with a broken leg. But not Alex. He'd rather poke the fracture, ask if it hurt, and then smirk when the person writhed in pain.

A small voice inside me said I was the same. How many times had I said something just to watch someone else squirm? Like the time I'd started the rumor that a girl at school had given Alex a blow job behind the gym during lunch. Granted, she'd made fun of deaf people, but she hadn't, as far as I knew, touched Alex, let alone anything more. What was her name anyway? She transferred after the rumor hit full throttle.

Or the time I let my brother take the fall for stealing stuff from my parents when I knew who'd really done it.

Alex.

And I'd helped him.

Maggie waved goodbye, and I turned back to my room. To

my jewelry box. My favorite necklaces had been hanging on a rack screwed into the wall, and it had been ripped out, leaving holes in the drywall. The wooden box that normally sat on my dresser below the rack was in two pieces in the middle of the room with the bent rack on top.

I picked my necklaces out of the pile, laying them in the lid of a shoebox I'd snagged from the closet. Earrings went into the top half of a broken gold soccer ball that had been part of my MVP trophy from last fall's varsity team. Now it formed the perfect cup.

A few minutes later, I had two piles of jewelry. My silver lightning bolt was there. The random fashion necklaces my mother had given me over the years were intact. But something felt off. I was missing something.

The locket. Maggie's Christmas gift to me. It was gone.

I pulled my phone out of the pocket of the jacket I'd worn to the funeral and sent a message to Penetr8er.

Not funny, Alex.

The reply was instant. *Oh?*

I found your "present." And you stole my necklace. My fingers slid through the pile of necklaces as if I'd find the missing locket if I just checked again.

I powered my phone off before I had a chance for my fingers to type out anything more. Creep.

Memories of my bed, clad in its in red comforter, called to me. But instead of my usual oasis, or fortress of solitude as Gin would call it, everything was a war zone in here.

A war with my desire to bring Alex to justice on one side of the battlefield, and the hope to not destroy the rest of my friends in the process on the other.

TWENTY-THREE

SATURDAY EVENING

I paced from one side of Paisley's bedroom to the other. It was ten steps from the edge of her turquoise-and-yellow explosion of a bedspread to the window looking out to the street. She sat on a beanbag chair, her eyes pinging back and forth like a cartoon cat as she watched me.

"You can sit down," she said.

"I can't. If I sit down, I'll explode."

"Besides, Harper is like an object that's never at rest," a voice said from the doorway. I spun around. Benji.

"Easy, killer," Benji said. We all flinched at the word, and he looked apologetic as he walked sideways across the room until he reached Paisley. He sat down next to her and she immediately leaned into him. He put his arm around her shoulder.

I started pacing again. "How do we deal with this?" My voice pulsated with anger.

"We can always tell the truth," Paisley said in a soft voice. Like she was afraid I'd explode on her instead of wearing holes through her bright yellow area rug.

"We'll get in trouble," I said.

"Maybe we deserve to."

I slowed as the impact of Paisley's words sunk in, but then I resumed my pacing. "Alex deserves to pay for breaking into my room. But more importantly, we need to figure out how he was involved in Sarah's death. Maybe the overdose was an accident. But what if it wasn't?"

"I'm only worried about Sarah," Paisley's voice had grown stronger, like she'd gained an espresso shot of confidence.

"If it was an accident, there has to be a way to bring Alex to justice without blowing up all of our lives." My words sounded wrong to my ears, but I couldn't figure out how to say what I meant. I couldn't risk Gin's future on my hunch. Paisley and Benji also didn't deserve to suffer the consequences if I was wrong. Tearing my hair out would be easier than thinking.

The doorbell rang. "That's probably Gin. I'll let him in." Paisley looked relieved to escape her bedroom.

My hand went to my hip pocket. Alex's "present" was inside. What was I supposed to do with it, and what could he possibly want with my locket? What game was he playing? As I whirled around, I caught Benji's eyes. He held his hands out like you do to calm down an irrational person. "Can you please try to chill?"

"What's your cousin thinking?" I asked. I stared at him, tracing the similarity between Alex and Benji. They were about the same height, although Alex's body was muscular from basketball and weight training, while Benji just looks gangly. Same brown hair. Same eye shape. But Benji didn't have that hard-to-pinpoint but ever present air of cockiness that permeates the room whenever Alex enters. It's easy to forget about Benji, to let him fade into the background, even when you know he's there. If Alex is a roar in a canyon, Benji is the echo that comes back a moment later.

"Why are you staring at me?" Benji asked. "And how would I know what Alex is thinking? Sarah's death hit him hard. He's all over the map, from grief to not wanting to admit how much he cared."

I shook my head and paced across the room again. I opened my mouth but the sound of three different people outside the door made my lips go mute.

"Hi, everyone!" A blond woman came in with Gin and Paisley.

"Everyone, this is my Aunt Jane. She's here for a few days."

"I just wanted to ask if y'all need anything," Aunt Jane said.

Her twangy voice reminded me of Paisley's mom. "I know it's been a rough day for y'all."

"We're fine," I said.

"Harper." Gin gave me the be-polite look he's been practicing for the past decade. "Thank you, Ms. Clay. If we need anything, we'll ask."

"Call if you need me," she said and slowly left, like she didn't want to leave all of us alone. Like we'd get into a big orgy or something if we were left in a bedroom without adult supervision.

"Her last name isn't Clay. She's my mom's sister—"

"It doesn't matter, Paisley," I interrupted.

"Harper, be nice," Gin said. "It's been a rough day for all of us, not just you. You don't need to take Paisley's head off."

"Sorry, Pais," I said, and she gave me a small smile in return.

"So your parents are out of town or something?"

"Yeah, my parents are at a trade show for their company. Long story. They didn't want to leave me alone after what happened with Sarah, so Aunt Jane came down to stay."

"What they think happened to Sarah," I said.

"You don't have any proof that Alex hurt Sarah," Gin said. "I overheard my parents talking, and her death was ruled an accident."

"Fine, let's rehash the argument. Sarah Dietz. Did you really think she'd commit suicide? Was she stupid enough to OD?"

Gin reached out to grab my hand as I paced by him, but he let it go when I pulled it away. "No," he said.

"You guys?" I looked at Benji and Paisley. They both shook their heads in response.

"You can't prove Alex broke into your house," Benji said.

I stopped and stared at him. "Why, did you break in? Did you tell me to 'look for your present' and then leave one of Sarah's necklaces in my room after trashing it?"

Paisley and Benji both flinched. Paisley looked at her hands.

"Chill for a moment, Harp." Gin stepped over to me and put his hand on my shoulder. I glared into his eyes and he gave back as good as he got, except he had his be-reasonable expression versus the look of pure fury I had been directing at him. I deflated slightly, and he patted my shoulder. Taking my anger out on Gin wouldn't help anything.

"Should we turn ourselves in?" Paisley asked, the tone of her voice getting higher at the end of the sentence.

"If we do, I won't get into MIT and you can forget about any good design school, Pais," Benji said.

Gin quit looking me in the eye and turned to Benji. "Are you seriously weighing getting into a good university against Sarah's death?"

"Exactly!" Finally Gin was agreeing with me.

"Please don't help," Gin muttered at me. I flung my arm out to punch him on the shoulder, but he grabbed my hand and gave it a gentle squeeze. I went limp at the unexpected gentleness.

"You're right." Benji held his hands up in surrender. "Justice for Sarah should trump petty things like the rest of our lives."

"It's not petty," I snapped back. "How can you defend him? Sarah is dead. It's not like he just dumped her or something."

I paced across the floor. Not turning Alex in would keep all of us from getting into trouble. But what was the cost of Alex going free? The thought picked at the back of my mind, rubbing against a sore spot, like an ill-fitting pair of sandals in summer. But a Band-Aid and dab of Neosporin won't bring Sarah back to life.

"When we started this whole thing," I said slowly, "we made

rules. We followed them. But death was never part of the bargain. We can't just let it go."

Paisley met my gaze. Her eyes were full of tears again, and her hands shook. She looked like she felt trapped, and not just 'cause she had Benji on one side of her and me bearing down on her on the other.

"None of us like this decision," I whispered to her. Maggie. If I got into trouble, who'd look after her? But how could I look her in the eyes if I didn't confess?

Benji groaned and put his hands over his ears. He dropped his hands and looked around the room. "Let me try again. Is there any way to turn him in that doesn't risk ruining our futures? Let's say I believe you and Alex was somehow responsible for Sarah's death, accident or not. You know if we turn Alex in, he'll rat all of us out."

Paisley nodded along as Benji spoke. "Alex would torpedo all of us," she added.

My mind was whirling. "So you're saying that we need proof that Alex did it. Something that means no one will worry about the burglaries even if he tries to twist this back around on us."

"If he did it," Paisley said.

My eyes snapped back to Paisley. She looked down so she missed my grim half smile. "So you're saying we need to get him to confess."

"How do we trick him into that?" Benji asked me.

"He's your cousin. Don't you have the inside scoop?" I asked.

Benji shrugged. "You're forgetting one key thing: Why would Alex have done it? If he was tired of Sarah, he would have just dumped her. He'd done that to other girls."

"That's a good point," Gin said, and I turned to glare at him. He stared back. "It's the truth, Harper."

"It's not like Sarah always made smart decisions," Benji said.

Paisley sent a watery smile in my direction. "Like picking a fight with you at soccer practice," she said.

My half smile in response was grim. "That whole incident was stupid."

"Yeah, you left intense bruises," Benji said and pointed to his abdomen, sort of center and a few inches to the left, and to his ribs. "You can punch."

"There's something else, you know," Paisley said. Her voice had grown steadier as she looked at me. "Just because we didn't think Sarah would do drugs on her own doesn't mean she was clean. You know how easily people can hide it. Maybe we all missed the signs, and it was an accident. Alex could just be going off the rails."

Benji sighed. "It's not the best answer, but I think we should wait a few days. One of us should talk to Alex in the meantime. If we still think he killed Sarah after the shock has worn off, or when we find proof, we call the detective. But for now, sit tight. Especially you, Harper—try to keep your head. You won't help anyone, including yourself, if you go off on Alex."

Gin put his arm around my shoulders as I stepped forward. "I'll make plans with Alex and get him to talk about Sarah. I'll see if I can get him to confess. You know he's cocky, and I can use that," he said. He pulled me against him like he was afraid I was going to attack Benji.

I tried to shrug his arm off my shoulder, but he squeezed tighter. "Chill for a moment," he mumbled into my ear. He turned his head away. "What do you think, Paisley?"

"I don't know what to do. Taking a few days and seeing if we can get Alex to confess makes sense. Everything feels like I'm looking at it through one of those vintage kaleidoscope things. Nothing is where it should be," she said. She looked down at the throw pillow in her lap, twisting the ends of its tassel around her fingers. She'd lost her weepy look in favor of a combination of troubled and thoughtful.

"Fine," I said. "Fine. I'll wait for two days. I'm looking forward to saying I told you so." I wheeled around, knocking Gin's arm off me as I turned. I left.

"Harper!" Paisley called after me. "Be sure to check SchoolFriends!"

———

I paced in the hotel room. Eight steps across and eight back. My father had loaded all of us up when I got back from Paisley's, saying we couldn't stay at home. Too messy.

Maggie looked at me from the bed next to the window. We were in a two-bedroom suite complete with in-room minibars. She was eating a bag of potato chips and had a chocolate bar in front of her. Dinner of champions.

"You okay?"

"Fine."

I paused by my backpack, which had escaped the burglary 'cause

I'd left it in the trunk of Mom's car on Friday afternoon. I pulled my tablet out and flopped on the other bed.

A few clicks and I'd accepted the twenty-dollar charge for twenty-four hours of Wi-Fi. A few more, and I was entering my login info for SchoolFriends.

More posts about Sarah. About how people were going to miss her. My fingers stilled and I quit scrolling.

Someone had posted Sarah's obituary from the newspaper:

Sarah Dietz passed away at age sixteen. She was loved by many, including her parents, Joe and Emily, and her brother James. Sarah was a junior at Stonefeld High School and was a member of its varsity soccer team. She also played club soccer, maintained a 3.6 GPA, and was active in the Communications Club. She wanted to be a journalist.

My eyes blurred but a few blinks cleared them up. What else could they really say? My grandfather's obituary had mentioned his career as an attorney and listed his children, grandchildren, and a wide variety of achievements. What had Sarah achieved? What had I?

I scrolled down and my whole body tensed. Someone had uploaded photos from Sarah's funeral, including one of me. I looked like I was holding back tears, but I hadn't been that upset during the funeral. Or had I? Maggie was out of focus behind me, her hair catching the sunlight in a red blurry glow.

Then I read the caption: *Someone is faking friendship. Bee Otch.*

My eyes snapped to the name that had posted. Taylor Durnhap? Who was she? The blond-haired girl in the photo looked like a toothpaste ad. Big white teeth. Pink scoop-neck T-shirt.

I typed in a response but then deleted it. Telling her where to go wouldn't help me with Mr. Jeffries, and I was too angry to think of an alternative way to spell the words so it wouldn't trigger the school's filter.

I pulled my phone out of my pajama pocket and texted Paisley. *Who's Taylor Durnhap and how to do I find her?*

Paisley response came seconds later. **That's just it. I don't think that's the real Taylor.**

It's her account.

I paced across the floor again. Maggie rolled to face away from me.

Paisley responded: **But not her photo. Taylor's Black. And a boy.**

I almost typed back **So who wrote this?** But I knew the answer. *Alex.*

TWENTY-FOUR

JULY: NINE MONTHS AGO

The smell of the black Sharpie in my hand made me feel a bit nauseated, but I continued drawing a Superman logo on the red cast in front of me. Gin's left leg was propped up on an ottoman, freshly plastered in a cast that ran from just below his knee and encompassed his ankle. There was an inch of knee showing between his cast and dark blue cargo shorts.

"I have a Crashing Man sticker I can donate to the cause," I said nodding at the cast. "It'd be perfect."

"So thoughtful of you."

I smiled at the sarcastic tone in Gin's voice and kept drawing. "Oh, poor Gin!" Paisley said as she and Benji walked through the kitchen into Alex's living room.

"It's a broken leg, not an incurable disease," Gin said but accepted Paisley's hug when she carefully lowered herself to wrap her arms around him, as if he was something delicate that would break if she touched too hard or grabbed too quickly.

"Hey, man," Benji nodded from behind Paisley and walked over to stare out the sliding glass door to the backyard. "You need anything? Coke? Bourbon?"

"Cokes would be good," I called back.

There was another knock at the door, but footsteps headed to the door while Benji's head was in the fridge, playing host in his uncle's house. After a few clinks, he pulled out two bottles of Coke and a beer.

"Hey, Mr. Conway," Sarah's voice carried down the hallway, and the flirty uptick in her voice made my hands still. Her next words were only a murmur, followed by a deep laugh, then a giggle. Mr. Conway's smile as he followed Sarah into the room made me feel like cold fingers were running down my back. I turned back to focus on Gin.

Sarah paused to pull the beer out of Benji's hand and gave a matching flirty look to both Mr. Conway and Benji. I rolled my eyes and turned back to Gin's cast.

"There's rum and peach schnapps too, if you want to make a drink for the girls," Mr. Conway told Benji.

"Can you imagine my mom saying anything like that?" Gin murmured to me.

I snorted. "My mother doesn't share."

Paisley brought the Cokes over to us, leaving them on the side table next to Gin. She paused by me and whispered in my ear "You know that Benji's dad is in a hospital in Cleveland, right? He went to see someone that's like the best heart doctor in the nation."

"That's…too bad," I said, and she straightened up. I went back to my Sharpie art.

The front door opened again, and I could feel Alex's presence as he walked down the hallway. He paused behind me. "Tough luck," Alex said as he looked down at Gin's broken leg.

"How long will you be out?" Sarah sounded overly sympathetic, like she'd just swallowed an instruction manual on how to be nice to people.

"The cast should come off in six weeks. Little PT and I'll be back in no time," Gin said.

"How'd you bust it?" A smug smile spread across Alex's face as he asked, like he already knew. I stopped myself from jamming the Sharpie into his leg.

"This will shock you but during a soccer game." Gin picked up his bottle of Coke and took a drink. Like this happened every day.

"Slide tackle gone wrong?" Alex followed up. I gave him the stink-eye, and he gave me a broad smile in return.

"No, I was taken down by a pothole," Gin said.

"Gotta hate it when the field strikes back," I said.

Gin flashed me his grin, the special one he only gave to me. The one that said we were fellow conspirators, aligned. I smiled back.

"I'm taking off," Mr. Conway told Alex and Benji. "Don't do anything too stupid."

"Like you'd need to worry," Alex said. "Especially with Benji around acting all adult."

"I know our little Benji is the responsible one," Mr. Conway said, there were a few notes of pride in his voice, but the condescending undertone made my back stiffen.

Mr. Conway paused for a second, so I said "Bye" and gave him a cheery smile and waved like I was a contestant in a beauty pageant, or one of the girls who rode on the back of a classic car around the football field when it was homecoming.

Like I'd done last year and our freshman year.

Gin laughed as the front door shut after Alex's dad. "Harper!" he said.

I tried to give him an innocent smile, but I could feel the right side of my mouth jerking up like it always did when I was sarcastic.

The room was silent for a moment. I capped the Sharpie and turned to face the room and leaned against the side of Gin's chair. He ran his fingers through my hair and I let him do it for a second before turning back to face his cast again. "So what's going on, Cuz? What do you want to talk about?" Benji asked. I glanced his way; his T-shirt said *Luckily My Army of Deadly Robots Understands Me.* He looked at Alex with a raised eyebrow.

"So, guys," Alex said in a loud voice, causing everyone to turn and look at him, "I have an idea."

"No, I'm not going to Sadie Hawkins with you. Besides, the girl's supposed to ask," I said.

Sarah glared at me. "I'm going to ask him." She moved so her shoulder brushed against Alex's side. Marking her territory.

"Good for you." I laughed, pausing for my hand to become steady again before completing the final line on my drawing. I had sketched a hand making a series of signs. I looked up at Gin wondering if he'd catch on.

"What does that mean?" Paisley said, inspecting my artwork from over my shoulder. "Are you telling everyone he's a hero? 'Cause he totally is."

"Thanks, Pais," Gin laughed. My snort sounded more like a cough as I read his cast. My artwork was rough, but anyone who knew ASL would be able to tell it was the signs for "dumb ass." With a broken leg, we weren't going to be able to do any of the things we'd planned to do in the final weeks of summer. No swimming. No geocaching with Maggie. No training runs in the park as we geared up for fall soccer. Netflix and books were in Gin's future. If I was in the mood, I might fetch him drinks or chauffeur him around town.

Benji said, "C'mon, guys, listen to Alex—" but his voice was drowned out by his cousin.

"Seriously, guys," Alex interrupted.

"Oh, someone's on the rag," I said. Gin snorted, making me wonder how strong his painkillers were 'cause that wasn't a funny insult.

"I have an idea for a game we can play. All of us," Alex glanced around the room. Sarah, like always, was staring at Alex with a lovesick puppy expression. Her eyes were big and focused on his every word. Paisley raised an eyebrow at me, and Benji had a what's-all-this-about look on his face.

Gin definitely looked high.

"As long as it's not spin the bottle," I said.

Alex snorted. "That's kids' stuff. I'm thinking of something more dangerous. More fun. Less junior high."

Gin nudged me with the foot of his good leg. "I'll play spin the bottle with you. But just you."

"Like you need a bottle for that," Sarah muttered.

"You're one to talk," I said.

"Girls, girls, my idea will also give you a way to channel all of that aggression!" Alex's voice boomed out, covering our squabbles and side conversations. Paisley quit whispering to Benji.

"Okay, Alex, what's your idea?" Paisley's voice had her patented peacemaker tone.

"You know Paisley is going out of town next month?" After everyone nodded, Alex continued. "So one of us should burglarize her house while she's gone."

Paisley snorted. "No, really, what's your idea?"

"Paisley, my little fashionista, I'm serious!"

"Really, Alex," I said. "You think we should break into Paisley's house?"

"I think one of us should," he said. "But just one at a time. We'll all get a chance to go since all of our families will vacation or leave town at some point. It will be a challenge. We'll see who can keep their nerve. Who freaks out like a little girl and runs away."

"What do we steal? And what would we do with it?" I asked.

"We steal whatever and then sell it. People do it all the time. I'm sure we can figure it out."

"I'm sure no one would notice we're stealing their stuff. Maybe we can just have a garage sale. I'll put up signs," I said.

"In the city, Harper. There are pawn shops."

"You know how to fence stolen goods?" Gin asked.

"Listen to you. That *Law & Order* marathon you watched last month is paying off. Sounds like you actually have some street cred," I said.

Gin looked down at me. "I have lots of street cred, baby."

I snorted. "Closest you've ever been to 'the projects' involves science class. And it was an in-class experiment."

"Huh?" Gin said. He blinked and I studied his pupils for a moment. They were too big.

"Wouldn't you get in trouble? We have an alarm that will be set while we're gone," Benji said.

Alex shrugged. "It wouldn't be worth doing if there wasn't some risk. But we all know our alarm codes and can make spare keys."

"I'll do it. I'm brave," Sarah said. She gave me the stink-eye, which made her nose scrunch up like a three-year-old with constipation.

"It's not fear that's making me question this," I said.

"Maybe we should all take a moment to think this through," Benji said.

"Be nice," Paisley said. "Let's be honest—I don't want any of you stealing stuff from my room."

"That's easy to fix," I said. "We could make rules, like no stealing from each other."

"So Harper's on board," Benji said.

"I didn't say I'm in." I shook my head. "I just said we could make ground rules."

"Then let's think this through," Benji said. "I'll get some paper." He brought over a pad of paper and a pen from the kitchen. "Okay," Benji said and sat down on the floor by the coffee table. He wrote *Ground Rules* on the paper.

"First rule: no stealing from each other," Benji said as he wrote it down.

"Nothing too unique. Nothing inherited, or—"

"Irreplaceable," Gin said.

"Good," Benji said. "Keep it coming."

They talked for a while, but my eyes were drawn to Gin, who was leaning back in his chair, staring at the ceiling. "You need to go home? How are you feeling?" I asked him softly.

"Kinda floaty," he said.

I patted his knee on the uninjured leg, like I was his grandmother or something.

I turned back to the group. "No one steals from Maggie," I said.

"What's that?" Benji looked up from his list. Alex turned to me with his usual cocky smile. Paisley raised an eyebrow, and Sarah flipped her hair dismissively.

"If you break into my house, you don't steal from Maggie. Let's put that in the rules. No siblings without permission."

"What about your parents?" Sarah asked, her snooty-girl voice in full force. I scowled at her.

"Screw them. But I'll fuck you up if you mess with Maggie."

MONDAY AFTERNOON: APRIL 18

"How're you doing?" Gin asked me as I organized my bag after my last class of the day.

"Oh, you know, brilliant." I straightened up, grimacing at the weight of my bag as I picked it up off the floor.

"Did you see you-know-who?"

"The Antichrist? No, didn't lay eyes on him. Was he even at school?"

Gin shrugged and started to turn down the hallway opposite the direction to the parking lot.

"Why are you going that way?" I asked.

"Don't you remember? We're driving Benji home," Gin said and resumed walking down the hallway. I followed like a duckling following a full-grown duck. Or six-foot soccer player in this case.

"Can you believe Coach didn't cancel any practices because of Sarah? He said we'd honor her memory by continuing."

"But you never have club practice on Mondays, so why are you worried about practices later this week?" Gin stared straight ahead.

I sighed. Maybe I should try quacking. Maybe that'd break through whatever barrier Gin had thrown up, because I'd clearly said the wrong thing. Whatever. He can deal. So can my coach, although I still don't get how playing and practicing like normal serves her memory. Sarah would rather see us dressed in black protesting that we can't kick a soccer ball again without the memory of her causing us to shrivel up in pain.

Benji was talking with a couple of guys as we approached. They were all dressed like Benji in geek-chic clothing. I could see Paisley's style in Benji's button-down shirt and brown shoes. The others were more geek, less chic. Add in Benji's height—the same as his cousin Alex, although I always think of Benji as being shorter—and he could be king of his domain. Maybe if he keeps listening to Paisley.

"Hey." Benji was in full nonchalant mode when we walked up. His shoulders were relaxed, his entire being seemed to say, "Check me out; I'm cool." Maybe he's picked up more from Alex than I thought. His orange jacket with navy-blue stripes was over one arm.

"You ready?" Gin's voice was calm, friendly, but the set of his shoulders told me he was still fighting some sort of inner battle. What set him off?

Did I even want to deal with this? Except Mom had my car since hers was in the shop. Since we were giving Benji a lift, clearly I couldn't try to go get a ride with Paisley instead in her bright yellow Bug. Which was sad 'cause usually I could get her to let me drive by pretending I loved her eyesore of a car, even though I really just didn't want to see her run stop signs and drive too close to the side of the road. So where was she anyway?

"Yeah, I'm ready," Benji said. "See you guys tomorrow."

"Bye, dude."

Benji fist-bumped his friends.

Dude? Who calls people *dude*? And he wasn't even being ironic.

"So what crawled up your ass?" I asked Gin as the three of us headed toward the Jeep.

"What do you mean?"

"You seem edgy."

Gin shrugged, his shoulder muscles knotting up under his hooded sweatshirt. His brown eyes looked over my head. It reminded me of the time Paisley brought a puppy over to Gin's house, and his Lab ignored the puppy even though it jumped up and down in front of it. Murphy the Lab just looked at the wall above the puppy, as if it was below his notice.

If Gin thought I was going to dance for his attention, he had another thing coming.

"Shotgun," Benji said as we walked up to the Jeep.

I turned to him, giving him my drop-dead-loser look, and he recoiled.

"Fine, you can sit in front," he muttered. I held the front seat forward so he could crawl inside. His knees bumped against the front seats as he sat in the middle of the back seat, his head practically poking through the bucket seats. I was tempted to pat him on the head and offer him a treat if he was a good boy and didn't slobber on me.

Gin turned his radio to a hip-hop station, his fingers pounding along with the beat as he navigated out of the parking lot. He was practically wearing a neon sign that blinked "don't talk to me."

"Why are we going this way?" Benji shouted from the back.

"We're picking up Maggie," I said.

"Ah."

Maggie broke into a grin when she saw the Jeep, although the smile faltered when she saw that she was sharing the back seat. I signed "Talk later" before I let her into the back with Benji.

My sister nodded at Benji, who nodded back from his new spot behind Gin. "I should have insisted on shotgun," he said. "I can't talk to your little sister."

"You can try to talk to her. She's getting good at reading lips and can use the practice." I turned and faced forward.

"Harper, can you please be nice for once and switch with Benji? He's too tall for the back seat, and, besides, Maggie might like to talk with you."

"Fine." A quick switch and Maggie was behind Gin while I was behind Benji, who smirked at me as Gin pulled out of the parking lot and headed down Grant Street. I "accidentally" kicked the back of Benji's seat a few times.

We skirted around downtown on our way back to our neighborhood. Traffic slowed and I glanced up at the hospital and medical center, which overlooked downtown like a warped castle. Traffic was stopped coming downhill from it.

"This sucks," Benji muttered. "I bet Paisley's stuck too. She had some doctor's appointment today and left school early."

"Yeah, everything's stopped," Gin said.

Eventually, traffic started to inch forward and Gin merged over when a police officer directed our lane. As we came to the traffic light linking the medical center with downtown, my heart stopped.

TWENTY-FIVE

MONDAY AFTERNOON, CONTINUED

"Shit." Gin's Wrangler came to a stop as we stared at the accident. Bright yellow Bug with a crumpled front end and destroyed front windshield. It looked like the entire top of the car had been stepped on by a giant. Glass covered the ground around it. A semi was next to it, barely rumpled.

The police officer whistled and motioned Gin forward, but he didn't react. He just stared at the accident. A car honked behind us.

"Paisley!" Benji flung the door open and stumbled out toward the accident. He tried to run to the Bug, but a police officer grabbed him.

I shoved the seat forward and wormed out of the Jeep and

followed Benji. I put my hand on his shoulder. "Benji, we don't know it's her."

"That's her car. Look at the license plate."

"You two need to go back to your car," the police officer said.

"That's his girlfriend's car," I said. My heart thumped in my ears. Please don't let that be Paisley. There are other yellow Bugs in the world.

"I'm sorry, but you can't be here." His voice turned a little bit gentler, but it was even more firm. "Please return to your car."

I put my hand around Benji's elbow. "C'mon, Benji. We can't do anything here." He let me pull him back to the Jeep.

His face was dazed, like he wasn't sure where he was.

Please, please not Paisley.

Silence. Benji looked shell-shocked as he climbed into the back seat. He didn't even try to fight me for the front.

"I'm going to drop you off first," Gin told me after I climbed in and shut the door. "I don't want to leave Benji alone until we find out what happened. Any chance you have his mom's number?"

"Nah, but maybe my mother does. I'll text her and ask," I said and pulled out my phone and texted my mom. Traffic was slow until we hit the entrance to the neighborhood. We sped up to fifteen miles per hour and part of me wanted to tell Gin to slow down.

"We're not sure it's Paisley. Could it have been someone else? That's a popular car, right?" But I didn't believe the words even as they left my mouth. I couldn't even hope. Gin shrugged.

My phone dinged. My mother had come through with Benji's mother's number, along with *y?* I forwarded the number to Gin and put my phone back in my bag.

"Just sent you the phone number you asked for," I said.

Why did I sound like I had a giant stick up my ass?

Paisley. Maybe she's in the hospital fighting for her life.

Please be okay, Pais. Please.

Gin pulled up in front of my house. I looked at him, at the tense lines across his face. He leaned over and kissed me. "I'll call in a bit."

"Let me know if you hear anything." I glanced at Benji. He was staring at the back of my seat, his entire face closed off.

"C'mon, Mags." Gin jumped out of the car and held the seat open for her as she crawled out.

"What's going on?" She signed at me.

"Tell you in a bit."

Gin waved at Maggie before pulling away. Benji was still immobile in the back seat. Desolate. An island in and of himself.

Maggie pulled on my arm until I looked at her. "What happened?"

"The yellow car that wrecked was Paisley's."

"Is she okay?"

"We don't know."

Maggie lagged behind me on the walkway to the house. I wanted to do something, anything, rather than go inside and pretend to do my homework or watch TV.

Better get this over with. I pulled my house key out of my bag and slowly opened the door. The front entryway had been mopped, and the whole area looked shiny, new. Like a bunch of house elves had spent all day here.

"We're here."

"Took you long enough," my mother called back from the direction of the living room.

"Bad traffic."

"It's fine if you stop on the way home, just remember to text!"

"Whatever."

"I ordered pizza. It'll be here any time," my mother called after us as Maggie and I climbed the stairs.

"Delightful!" It wasn't even four p.m., way too early for dinner. Not that I'd ever be hungry again. Part of me wished for soccer practice and the chance to run around and forget everything, except we didn't have practice until Thursday.

I dumped my bag on my desk. I could go downstairs, but then I'd have to watch my mom spend quality time with her wine bottle. My eyes flickered to the drawer where I keep my running gear. Maybe a hard run was the answer. But what if Gin called with news and I didn't hear my phone?

The lemony scent of the detergent filled the air as I flopped onto my bed, causing me to wrinkle my nose. I wondered if Maggie's room had been laundered, vacuumed, and organized like mine had been. I glanced around; my bookshelves looked empty, the missing novels leaving large gaps. Would I be able to find my clothes? There's no way the cleaning service knew where everything was supposed to go.

My phone dug into my hip pocket, so I pulled it out and opened a browser. My fingers slowed as I typed in Paisley's blog.

She'd posted that morning, and I felt like my heart had been jerked out of my chest.

Instead of her usual photos, she'd filmed something. My finger hovered over the play button for a moment, and I swallowed before clicking.

"Hey everyone!" Paisley twirled in front of the camera. "Thanks for watching my first vlog! I'm having a giveaway in honor of this monumental event. Leave a comment to win this purse!"

She held up a yellow leather purse. "This was given to me by The Mothership, a local designer with an absolutely adorable boutique, to review on my blog. After using it for a few weeks, I can promise you it's…"

I tuned out just watching Paisley smile and talk. She looked so natural, like she was meant to talk about fashion on video. Her shiny pink lip gloss and purple eye shadow just screamed Paisley, as did her vintage high-waisted skirt and sweater set. She was beautiful.

"This purse looks like it's leather, but it's actually vegan and partially recycled…"

I smiled at the spirited sound in Paisley's voice. She was so vibrant, so alive.

"Next time, I'm premiering my new thrift-shop-finds feature, showing how I can get an entire outfit for less than twenty dollars!" The memory of her crumpled car flashed across my mind. The juxtaposition of it versus her bubbly blog post felt like a spike to my heart.

I was brushing a tear away from my eye when someone knocked on the door.

"What?" I called out.

"Can I come in?" my father asked as he opened the door.

"Okay." I swung my legs so I was sitting cross-legged on the bed instead of lying down. My eyes stopped watering as my back straightened. My body geared up for battle.

Dad was dressed in his suit from work. Charcoal pinstripes today with a light gray shirt. Very monochromatic, as Paisley would say.

Paisley.

He grabbed my desk chair and moved it so he was a few feet away from my bed and facing me. He sat down. I felt like I was in the principal's office.

Again.

"We heard about your friend Paisley. You drove past the accident?" Dad was solemn. I wonder if he looked like this when he fired his assistant at work last month.

"Uh-huh."

"Are you okay?"

"Is there any news? We saw her crumpled car, but the police didn't tell us anything."

"She didn't make it," Dad said. "She died in the accident. Are you okay?"

"Sound and in one piece. Unlike Paisley." I motioned to my body, focusing on the now to avoid falling into an abyss. There's no way Paisley is hurt. It had to be a different car.

Dad flinched. He loosened his tie and then messed with the cuff links at his wrist. "This isn't a joking matter."

"Who's laughing?" Paisley will when she comes home and finds everyone sad. My hands clenched.

"This has to be difficult for you. First Sarah, now Paisley. Do you want to talk about it?" He resumed fiddling with his cuff links.

"It's okay." My voice sounded small. I cleared my throat, but it wanted to close. Maybe Paisley really was gone. Maybe she wouldn't be at school tomorrow, ready to chatter about our English homework and be Paisley. Goofy, sweet Paisley. My father fidgeted like he wanted to go, and part of me wondered what he'd say if I told him I knew Alex was behind all of this. He had to be, although how could he have caused Paisley's accident? Could he have messed with her car? Maybe the brakes? Had he meant to kill her or just scare her? He talked about rebuilding cars with his dad. Could he also deconstruct them?

Guilt settled over me, trying to force the air out of my lungs. Even though I hadn't done anything to Paisley, my actions had snowballed into her death. I should have insisted we tell the police about Alex. If I told my dad right now, would he give me the looks he gave my brother, or would he call a lawyer to cover this up before he even had a chance to say he was disappointed in me?

"Such bad timing," Dad said. "First Sarah's overdose and then a fluke car accident. I wish you'd had time to grieve for one death before facing another."

"I'm more worried about my friends than myself." I heard an echo of Paisley in my words, which made me cringe. She'd been right when we talked about this at school after Sarah's death. We should have worried about Sarah first instead of worrying about getting into trouble. She'd been right. Too bad she wasn't able to say I told you so.

"Just know I can find a therapist for you if you'd like someone to talk to. Someone who specializes in grief."

"Thanks."

His eyes jolted toward me when he heard the sarcasm in my voice, but he just looked at me for a moment before standing up. He sighed. "If only Daniel had a fraction of your fortitude."

"Daniel's his own person. It's not like he doesn't take after at least one of his parents."

Dad stopped and turned back to face me. His eyes blazed. "What's that supposed to mean?"

"Like you haven't noticed Daniel and Mom are a lot alike?"

His shoulders relaxed from full-on argument mode into a medium-stress posture. "Don't talk nonsense," he said.

"Seriously?"

"I'll give you some leeway because two of your friends just died, but watch your mouth and don't talk about what you don't have the capacity to understand."

Ah, so he'd gone with the cold, I'm-smarter-and-in-charge manner of dealing with me. I narrowed my eyes; getting him to yell was more fun. Definitely better than feeling sad.

My phone beeped, distracting me. Dad walked out as I glanced down at my phone. It was Gin. *Going to Benji's. Want to come?*

I didn't have to think about it. *Yes.*

His response was almost instantaneous.

Be there in a few to pick you up. Unless you want to walk.

I typed back. *Come pick me up.*

TWENTY-SIX

Benji's dad let us in. "Thanks for coming over. Benji's in his room," he said, and he shuffled aside so we could walk up the stairs. He stood in the entrance of what was the office of my house, but it had been turned into a ground-level bedroom at Benji's after his father's first heart attack two years ago.

I followed Gin up the stairs, glancing around as we climbed. Photos of Benji and his family were spaced evenly up the staircase. Benji and Alex as kids. I paused by one of Benji and his mom visiting her family in London, posing in front of Big Ben with big smiles splashed across their faces.

Benji sat on a dark blue love seat in his room, his head in his hands. When he looked up, his eyes were red, but he wasn't crying.

"Hey guys." His voice was hoarse, but steady, and his hands shook as he picked up a mug from the small table next to him, but then he put it back down without taking a drink.

"I'll be back in a moment." Benji darted to his attached bathroom.

I glanced around Benji's room, digging his seating area with decked-out TV, love seat, and mini fridge. Wonder if I could convince my parents to do something similar in my room? The other side of his bedroom had a typical single bed with blue plaid comforter. A half-open door led to a walk-in closet. Standard boy room with an identical layout to Daniel's room at home.

Why was I thinking about this when I'd never see Paisley again?

I dropped into the navy-blue beanbag chair opposite the love seat, almost elbowing his Xbox in the process.

"Watch out," Gin said. He folded himself onto the floor next to me.

I shrugged. "Good thing I didn't take it out. He'd never recover from losing his girlfriend and his Xbox in one day."

"Harper—" Gin looked ready to argue, but there was a knock at the door. A sliver of guilt snaked through me.

Benji's mother bustled in with a tray. "I brought you tea," she said and put it down on the table by the love seat. She handed me a ceramic mug filled with a brown liquid. I took a sip. Sugar exploded on my tongue.

"I sweetened it 'cause you've all gone through a shock," she said. "Poor dears."

"Thank you," Gin said as he accepted the cup of tea. Benji rejoined us, sinking into the love seat while staring at the dark gray cross-trainers on his feet.

"Let me know if you need anything," she said and paused a moment while staring at Benji. She looked like she wanted to hug him, but she walked out instead.

I glanced at the tray, eyeing the plate of cookies, as I took a sip of the tea. It tasted like it was three parts sugar to one part tea. "Is that an English thing? Tea in times of tragedy?" I asked after she left, staring down in the murky brown depth of my cup.

"In my mom's world a cup of tea solves everything. Especially if it's laden with sugar for shock," Benji said.

Gin's smile was too grim to really look like a smile. "If only it was that easy."

"Are Paisley's parents back yet?" I asked.

"Flying home tonight." Benji stared at his carpet. "I should have driven her today."

"It wasn't your fault." I studied his downcast face. He must have the pattern on his gray-and-blue area rug memorized by now from the way his eyes studied it. But maybe he was seeing without thinking. Maybe his mind was filled with something else. Like visions of Paisley. The bright tone of her laugh and the way her hair swished when she giggled. How she always had a smile for everyone. How her humor would bubble out when you least expected it.

How she was such a great friend. How much he would miss her.

"Is there any chance Paisley's wreck really wasn't just an accident?" I asked.

Gin shrugged at me. "I don't know. I don't see how it couldn't be an accident. How could Alex have caused it? Why would he do it? But it's such a coincidence."

"He helps his dad rebuild cars, right?" The flashy red car that had been parked in Alex's driveway last summer flashed through my mind.

"He does. He's good at it too," Benji said. "I had to hang out with them talking carburetors and head gaskets last summer when my dad was in the hospital and I stayed with Alex."

"So maybe he messed with something in Paisley's car. Brakes, maybe? Something that would cause her to crash."

"But how could he have" Gin's voice trailed off.

"What?" I asked.

"There's no way to, well, make sure she died."

It was my turn to shrug. "Maybe that wasn't planned. Maybe he just wanted to scare her, scare us."

"You sound so callous," Benji said.

I told myself to stop talking as I remembered why we were here. First Sarah, now Paisley. Two girls I'd been around my whole life, and I'd never see them again. My friends.

I turned to him. "I'm sorry, Benji."

His shoulders shook like he was sobbing. But then he made a strangled gurgle of laughter. "If Harper Jacobs is being nice to me, I better take note," Benji gasped.

"I think we all know what to do," Gin said. I looked him straight in the eyes and he stared back without blinking. His brown eyes beamed resolution mixed with sorrow. Something within me answered. We needed to do what was right.

"Talk to the police?" I said. "Should we call them now?"

"Do you still have that detective's business card?" Gin's hand found my own. I gripped it back.

"Yeah, but it's in my backpack at home."

"Let's get it and then call him."

Benji's voice sounded hoarse again as he rejoined the conversation. "Let's do it tomorrow morning. I'd rather talk to him at school. I don't want to talk to him here. I can't disappoint my parents, not on top of them being sad about Paisley. They loved her. She helped my mom a lot, bringing groceries over and even helping with laundry."

"I didn't know that," I said, my voice small. I could picture Paisley bustling around the Conways' kitchen. She probably made retro food to match her style sense. She'd mentioned pimento mac and cheese once, although I'd never heard of pimento.

"So we'll call the detective once we get to school?" Gin asked, breaking me out of my thoughts.

Images of my father trying to stare down Detective Parker flashed through my mind. "Agreed. It'll be easier at school."

"So we're decided?" Gin's steady gaze moved from Benji to me to back to Benji as we both nodded. "I'll call the detective in the morning after we get to school."

"I'm sure we can use the principal's office to meet with him," I said.

"Since you're the principal's close personal friend and all." I turned to glare at Benji.

"What?" he said. "I thought you two exchanged Christmas presents. You're in there so much."

"Is this really the time to make jokes?" I asked. My control started to melt into anger.

"As if you're the one to criticize inappropriate comments."

"Your girlfriend just died."

"Both of you shove it," Gin snapped at us.

"You're right," I said to Gin. I stood up. "I should go. Benji—I'm really sorry about Paisley. Really."

"I know, Harper," Benji stood up and gave me an awkward hug. I patted his back twice before pulling away.

"Let's all ride to school together tomorrow," I said.

"Let's meet here," Benji said. "I'll need help convincing my parents I should go to school. They'll probably want me to stay home."

"Should we talk to them now?" Gin asked.

"Since sweet-talking parents isn't my superpower, I should go home." I stood, and Gin mirrored my movements. He tried to smile at me as he climbed to his feet.

I stepped up on my tiptoes and kissed him. "Tomorrow," I said. "This ends tomorrow." The words were a relief.

TWENTY-SEVEN

TUESDAY MORNING: APRIL 19

I gave up partway through the night and turned my iPad on low. If I wasn't going to float off to dreamland, at least my thoughts could have a soundtrack. My stomach felt like it was being twisted, and my whole body wanted to twitch. I'm pretty sure I could have counted all the sheep in New Zealand before falling asleep.

At six thirty, my alarm started to beep over the sound of a pop song. I bolted upright. My heart raced; I must have slid into sleep sometime after four a.m.

My body felt heavy as I stumbled toward the shower. The warm water did little to make me feel better even if my eyes felt like they could see more than a hazy version of reality. Hopefully, everything would clear up before we spewed out our confessions to the police.

What does one wear when they're planning on turning herself in to the fuzz? My usual faded boots and school khakis that fit my butt perfectly, for sure. Might as well add my favorite navy sweater since I'm sure to face a lifetime of prison jumpsuits after today. Too bad I have to start out the day in my school uniform. I wonder if I should wear my sweater with its discreet school logo for my mug shot. The school would adore having that photo on their website, advertising what an outstanding educational experience they gave students at the Academy. They loved to advertise students in the news.

I looked too preppy despite the dark shadows under my eyes, when I looked in the mirror, but oh well. I packed my undone homework in my bag. How many classes would we attend before talking to the detective? Okay, pretty much ready. Except for a quick glance around my room. When would I see it again? It wasn't the same as before Alex's attack, but it was rising from the ashes like a phoenix and was close to being normal. Well, normal enough.

Like me. Gin. Benji. We were going to rise from the ashes of Sarah and Paisley's deaths, even if this would be the end of life as we knew it. Alex was going to regret the day he messed with me. With us. My shoulders felt tense, so I straightened my back. There were a lot of truths I needed to tell, and not all involved Alex. Daniel deserved better from me. I owed him. One of his rehab programs insisted he make amends; now it's my turn.

I turned off the light and shut the door, pausing to touch the cut-out letters spelling my name that Maggie had made for my birthday last year.

How would I explain this to my little sister? I left a note on the bulletin board on her door that I was heading to Benji's house and that we'd pick her up at seven thirty. I ran over the plan Gin had last night: we'd meet at Benji's one last time to reassure each other to not freak out, and we'd go to school together.

It was almost seven a.m. I'd find something to do. Maybe take my last walk as a free woman.

"Harper."

My dad's voice made me stop in my tracks as I headed down the hallway toward the front door. I paused.

"Your mother and I talked, and we don't want you to go to school today. We're going to set up an urgent appointment with a grief counselor that my secretary knows."

Gee, thanks, Dad. Glad your secretary knows someone.

"We're also worried about you going to school here after losing two friends, so we're placing a call to your mother's old school—"

"Boarding school?" I said.

"And we think summer session there, followed by your senior year, would be a good change of pace. Keep you from brooding."

As if I'd ever leave Maggie. Except I was going to leave her by turning myself in. "Whatever. At least let me give Maggie a ride to school," I said. Even if I didn't meet up with the boys first, I could still turn myself in at the police station.

"I've already scheduled a cab for her."

"You've been busy."

"Yes, well, I need to get this taken care of so I can focus on some important matters later today."

Of course he did. His phone chimed and he answered it, walking in the direction of his home office.

My own phone dinged. Gin. *Parents don't want me to go to school.*

Ditto.

Meet at my house at 10? Gin responded.

Yes. I'd be able to sneak out before then.

I settled in to wait, hanging out with Maggie as she ate breakfast and caught her taxi. She kept looking at me with her eyes narrowed in worry but didn't say anything.

I waved as she caught her cab, and it was Dad's turn to leave about fifteen minutes later.

"Don't bother your mother. This all has been very hard on her," he told me as he pulled on an overcoat and then picked up his briefcase. "She's not feeling well this morning, so she's sleeping in."

"That's a change," I said.

"I don't have time for you to be smart. My assistant will call you when she sets up your appointment later today."

On that note, he exited to the garage, and I waited by the front door for his car to disappear around the block. I pulled my own coat from where I'd stashed it in the hall closet, along with my backpack, and slipped out the front door, closing it softly behind me, although I doubted my mother would have noticed if I'd slammed it.

A jogger in black tight Nike running pants with matching jacket passed me on the trail as I headed toward Gin's house. The trees were growing thick with leaves, and I bet the first May flowers were getting ready to sprout up.

I prefer the wildflowers of the trail system versus the manicured lawns with perfectly weeded beds of the neighborhood. Someone had tried to turn her front lawn into a vegetable garden with wooden planters last year, but everyone had freaked. My father had talked about how this was a breach of HOA regulations, scoffing at the argument that growing food was more important than appearances. "They can grow their carrots out of sight in the backyard," he'd complained.

Now my personal vegetable garden was going to be out for everyone to see. What would Dad say when he heard? He'd threatened to cut Daniel off several times, but he'd always picked up the pieces eventually. A grim smile crossed my face. Poor Dad. His handsome son struggled with drugs, his youngest daughter belonged to a world he'd never been willing to understand, and now the shining example of his success, his athletic, successful daughter, was going to be a felon before she turned seventeen. But it's okay. He has important shit to do this afternoon.

A car stopped for me at the crosswalk on Sunrise Crest, and I rejoined the trail on the other side of the street. Not too far to Gin's house, maybe three blocks. All of the houses on Turret looked over the gully.

My phone dinged, so I pulled it out of my pocket without thinking about it. Penetr8er. My lips curled into a snarl. Just wait, Alex. Your time has come.

I have something of yours.

My eyes riveted on the photo.

Maggie. With her hands and feet duct-taped in front of her. A matching strip of silver tape arced across her mouth.

My phone buzzed again.

I'll trade. You for Maggie. But if you go to the police your sister will die. You know I'll do it.

My fingers felt clumsy as I frantically typed. **What do you want?**

Go to the Strong Brew downtown. I'll text.

Another text popped up on my phone.

And Harper? This is just between me and you. Call anyone else and Maggie is dead.

I closed my eyes.

TWENTY-EIGHT

TUESDAY MORNING, CONTINUED

The Strong Brew, the corner coffee shop Gin and I had brought Paisley and Benji to less than a week ago, was bustling with people getting coffee to go. It felt like months had passed in that time.

I'd never get coffee with Paisley here again.

The idea of eating turned my stomach, but I forced myself to get in line to order an Americano and breakfast sandwich. Food would help me keep my strength up. My whole body felt tired, like it needed me to curl up in the corner and go to sleep for one hundred years. But that had to wait.

Only Maggie mattered.

There was an open table at the back and I slid into it with my coffee and freshly pressed panini sandwich. I'm sure the fresh egg and melted cheese was delicious. It could have been rat poison on cardboard for all that it mattered to me as I chewed automatically.

I stared at my phone waiting for Alex to message me. A trade. Me for Maggie. Hopefully, I'd have a chance to kick him in the balls after Maggie got away to safety.

Almost as if he'd known I'd been thinking about him, my phone pinged.

Go to Third and Grand.

Why? I glared at my phone.

Text me when you get there.

Nondescript office buildings surrounded me on the corner of Third and Grand. There was a blue mailbox on the corner and a newspaper box selling the daily paper from the city. A quick glance around told me the only thing else on the corner was a small shop selling candy bars and bad coffee to the offices around it.

My sister better be okay. I typed. **If you harm a single hair on her head, you're dead.**

Buy a newspaper. Check the top of the box.

The top of the box? There wasn't anything on top of the black metal box, so I pulled a few quarters from my bag and plopped them into the money slot. I opened the box.

I leaned over and looked at the top of the box but couldn't see anything. I ran my fingers across the top of the interior. Bingo. A quick twist and a manila envelope was in my hands.

I shut the box behind, ignoring the newspaper I'd paid for.

My fingernails were just long enough to tear through the tape holding the envelope shut. Inside was a simple black cell phone.

There was a text message waiting for me.

Did you buy the newspaper on the bottom of the stack?

No.

Silly girl. Go back.

My hands trembled slightly as I fed more quarters into the newspaper box, opened the door, and pulled out the newspaper on the very bottom of the stack. I pulled it out and the new phone dinged with a text message.

Turn off your iPhone.

I glanced at my phone. It felt like a buoy holding me to life.

Why?

Turn it off now or don't bother looking for Maggie. You'll never find her.

Fine.

Now leave it behind. Put it on top of the newspaper box.

Okay.

I slipped my phone back into my pocket and kept the new phone in my hand.

Not in your pocket. On the newspaper box. Now.

I wheeled around, scanning the windows, cars, and pedestrians near me. No Alex. But he had to be watching.

Now.

I put my phone on top of the dark-green newspaper box, and I wanted to snatch it back.

Back away. Then open the newspaper.

I stepped back so I crossed the middle of the sidewalk and stopped by a red brick building. I slowly opened the paper and pulled out the yellow sheet of paper stuck inside.

TWENTY-NINE

I recognized the canary yellow sheet of paper. The tiny gift shop at the south entrance of Dry Hollow Park hands them out. There's a series of paths running through the park, including my favorite that curves around the soccer fields and looks down on them from above, and this map showed visitors the system. There was an X on the map in a wooded area near the archery range with the words "Maggie marks the spot." My phone beeped.

Come find me. I'll be waiting.

My teeth ached as I clenched them. ***Hurt Maggie and I'll kill you.***

I glanced at my mobile phone sitting on the newspaper box, but then I glanced around again. Where was Alex hiding? Could he still see me?

Even though I wanted to grab my phone, I forced myself to take a step toward the bus stop on the opposite corner of the street. When the light for pedestrians turned green, I watched my brown boots as I strode across the intersection.

"Watch it!"

My eyes snapped upward when a guy in a business suit and trench coat ran into me, a mobile phone in his hand.

"You could try paying attention too," I told him, and he scowled at me. I glared back, feeling a warm ball of anger gather inside me. It was like a jolt of caffeine on an empty stomach, except instead of awake, I felt ready to attack the world.

The man in the suit walked on, and the anger continued to give a bounce to my step as I marched the rest of the way across the street. Alex thought he was in control, and he did carry the trump card with Maggie.

But I had my own advantage, like my knowledge of the park. Alex hadn't thought that part through. As I counted out change for the bus, I took inventory of what I had with me. One textbook and two notebooks. Several pens. A graphing calculator. A bar of chocolate. Half-empty water bottle. A seven-inch tablet.

I started to smile when I saw the tablet, but I slid the expression off my face in case Alex was still watching. I rooted around in my bag, pretending I was just finding one last quarter for my fare, but my mind was spinning with ideas. I paused when I saw a flash of orange out of the corner of my eye, and a brief moment of hope lit my chest. Was that Gin's Jeep? But it was gone around the corner. Maybe it wasn't even a Jeep.

The bus pulled up and as the wheels stopped in front of me, the gears in my head started spinning in overdrive.

"Shouldn't you be in school?" the driver asked as I dropped my change into the money collector.

"I'm doing a project at the park." I took my ticket out of his hand and headed to the back of the bus.

Alex had marked a spot off Dry Hollow's Oak Trail. I'd stay on the bus longer and enter the park from the south, instead of the closer north entrance.

I pulled the tablet from my bag. Maggie had a matching device, both given to us for Christmas. The city was running an experiment of offering Wi-Fi on buses and trains for commuters, and there was the blue symbol on the front windshield of the bus saying this bus was part of the pilot program.

After I logged on to my email, I popped open a new message and pulled the detective's card from my bag. Should I really send a confession before I got Maggie back?

Yes. I should.

My thoughts felt jumbled as I typed them out, and I had to correct words several times as I typed the wrong letters on the cramped screen. But twenty minutes later when the bus pulled up to the north end of the park, I had a coherent message explaining what we'd done, although I omitted Gin and Benji from the confession. I told him that Alex had Maggie and I was going to get her back. It wasn't the best essay I'd ever written, but my English teacher might be proud of my directness. Except she wouldn't like the content. I doubt she'd be down with criminal acts. After all, she doesn't even like sarcasm.

I quickly added Gin's father to the CC line and went ahead and added my dad too. I pictured how his face would look when he read the email. Despite my brother's drug problems, Daniel didn't have a criminal record. His one arrest had been sealed after the two R's: restitution and rehab. Now the glory child, the athlete, the one kid he could brag about, would be the scandal of the city. The cautionary tale to keep kids in line. There was once this girl, Harper, and she went from homecoming princess to felon in a single school year.

Hopefully, Gin's dad would keep his son out of the dung heap I was dragging myself into.

The black phone beeped.

Are you scared yet? Just you wait.

I shoved the phone into my bag and stared out the window. We passed by the east entrance, the one closest to the soccer fields. Maybe five more minutes until the south entrance of the park.

Until showtime.

I took a deep breath, glanced at the email one more time, and hit Send.

THIRTY

TUESDAY MORNING, CONTINUED

I pulled the yellow cord for the bus stop, and my boots hit the ground of the park with a determined thump. There were only a few cars in the parking lot. I paused by the gift shop, which was empty except for a white-haired volunteer wearing a rose-colored sweater. I pulled the tablet out of my bag and opened the voice recorder app and clicked it to record before slipping it into black mesh side panel of my bag. Hopefully, Alex wouldn't notice it. It should start recording when it heard voices. After refilling the water bottle from my bag, I was ready.

The trail from the gift shop headed uphill, but it would turn and go downward to reach the spot on Alex's map. I glanced at the map. It was just over two miles to Maggie.

I tightened the straps of my backpack and soldiered on.

The park was empty as I hiked along. No one played tennis on the courts even though the day was sunny and dry, plus cool enough to be perfect weather for a workout.

A rustling in the underbrush next to me caused me to wheel around, but there was nothing. Must be an animal. I've heard there are coyotes in the park. Plus raccoons. Squirrels. Nothing to worry about.

Quiet resettled on everything but the lack of noise means trouble is on the way. Like the brief moment of silence right before getting a week's worth of detention, but worse. The trail circled around the old playground with the swings. I wanted to check on the voice recorder nestled in my bag, but I needed to forget I had it. I had to have faith it would record everything I said. I needed to act natural. As natural as I could in this situation.

I needed to get Alex to confess.

Where are you? Alex asked.

On my way. I grimaced as a I wrote out the text. He was going to pay for kidnapping my sister.

Hurry. Maggie is waiting for you.

I didn't stop walking as I texted back. I slid the phone into my pants pocket although I wanted to throw it into the woods. The turret of the new playground came into view first, a castle in the daylight. Two small kids, one in a red jacket, the other in turquoise, played while two women chatted.

Just another mile.

The longest mile of my life.

Silence surrounded me. It was so quiet that it was like a thousand people screaming. The lack of noise felt deafening. The pounding of my heart was so loud I'm sure Alex could track me just by listening for it.

The trees became denser, and then I was there.

I stepped a few feet off the path into the trees. "Alex!" I shouted. "I know you're out there!"

Quietness reigned after the sound of my voice faded away. "Where are you, you bastard? If you've hurt Maggie, I'll massacre you!" I added.

"Really, Harper? You'll massacre me?" He emphasized *me* like he was amused. But the voice was wrong.

As I wheeled to the right, toward the voice, I knew.

The voice didn't belong to Alex. The tone was confident but lacked the cocky jauntiness that always colors his words.

There's only one person it could be.

But my ears have to be wrong. I trusted him. He'd never hurt Maggie.

THIRTY-ONE

TUESDAY MORNING, CONTINUED

"You?" I said.

"Expecting someone else?" Benji asked. The smirk on his face deserved a right hook. But there was something more important.

I stared at him, my eyes briefly going to the brick structure behind him before flicking back to him. Moss grew over the roof and down the sides of the building. A dark doorway led inside. I slid my backpack off my shoulders and left it in the shadow of a tree, hoping we were loud enough for the recorder to pick us up.

"Is Maggie inside?" I asked.

"Yeah, she's secure and cozy, all trussed up safely," he said. So many questions flew through my mind, competing with small details.

Why would Benji have killed Sarah? And what about Paisley? He'd loved her!

"The last thing I remember Sarah saying to you," I said, working through the memory while keeping an eye on Benji, "was that you should be happy to hang out with her, or something like that, and that she was with the fun cousin."

"Her actual quote? She said I should feel grateful to her. *Me* grateful to *her*. The skank."

His words smoldered with a bitter bite I'd never heard from Benji before. As if he'd wanted something she'd denied him. "You wanted her? Even though Paisley would do anything for you? And Sarah wouldn't give you the time of day, was that it?"

"You think you know it all, right Harper? Let me be the first to show you that you're an idiot. Me and Sarah? We'd been sleeping together for months, and she pulls that shit? Like she's better than me." Benji glanced off to the side for a moment. His eyes came back to me. "She had that in common with you. So much fake superiority. She liked to feel superior to Paisley by screwing around with her boyfriend."

A shudder went through me, but I saw the building behind Benji again. Maggie is in there. If she had seen him, he'd never let her go. Or me. But I didn't really matter. The important thing was to stall, to get him talking. "Why should I believe a word you're saying?"

"Ask Gin. He never told you about her, did he? About how Sarah threw herself at him when you weren't there."

His tone made me shiver, although the words weren't taking me to a happy place either. Who was this person? "Why did you do it?" I whispered.

"I just told you. What? You were expecting a big scene? Tears and recriminations? Grow up."

I thought about my parents, about how they never really fight in front of us, but also never really talked. Not to each other. Never to me. Did my father feel this level of contempt for my mother underneath his veneer of cool indifference? He'd sure lost faith in my brother when Daniel failed to become a reflection of success that made his parents look good.

"So you just, what, got rid of Sarah? What did you do, go to see her, got her drunk?"

"It was so easy. Easier than Sarah Dietz. Give her a drink from my flask. Lay her down for her final sleep. She thought I was apologizing. Being a sympathetic ear as she complained about you breaking into a house with Alex. I let her natter away. The way Gin lets you natter. She was such a broken record. Put a quarter in her and she'd complain about you."

A red-haired figure crawled out of the doorway behind us. Her hands were bound with duct tape, and her mouth was still covered. But my heart beat with joy. Maggie was alive. Mobile. I kept my face straight so Benji wouldn't look behind him.

"I can't believe you did all of this." I moved my hands, hoping Benji would think I was just gesturing random movements. "Run away. Now," I signed.

She shook her head no and raised her hands, which were taped together so she couldn't sign freely. But she could twist her hands enough to be clear.

"No." She added a head shake.

"Go get help."

She shook her head again and ducked down behind a tree, but I could see the edge of her head as she watched us. How could I get her to leave?

I stared at Benji to keep him focused on me, but I was surprised at the cocky lilt of his head. He now reminded me of his cousin and not of the robotics club member with his crew of brainiac misfits. "So you broke into my house," I said while I continued to sign to my sister. "Run away."

"Not leaving you," she signed back. "I can help."

"Leave. Get help."

Benji's smile made me feel like I'd been punched in the stomach. "No. I convinced Alex to do that. I needed to keep him busy. You really made him angry when you accused him of killing Sarah. Especially since he always thought the two of you had some sort of special thing going. I wonder where he got that idea."

"Like Silas," I said, suddenly enlightened. Silas. Paisley's old boyfriend who had so been so conveniently removed from the landscape of her life. "Go!"

"Very good, Harper. I've always known there's a bit of brain in there, even if you've never bothered to use it."

The sliver of Maggie I'd been keeping an eye on disappeared from sight, and the branch on a tree behind rustled. A small knot of tension loosened inside me; she'd finally listened. She'd better be on her way to safety. Now I needed to stall Benji to make sure my sister had enough time to get to safety. A fresh flame of resolve flickered through me as I stared at Benji. I spoke.

"You had Alex wrapped around your little finger."

"Pretty much. I prefer to see him as a puppet with me as the master."

"Did you get him to text me? Or was that your blathering?"

"Do you think I'd let him be in control and know that much? Especially something that'd give him leverage over me? I keep telling you. The secret to getting what you want is to keep your mouth shut. Keep the variables under your own control. But you just couldn't let Sarah's death go, could you? You never know when to let things be. Paisley would still be alive if you'd been able to keep your stupid mouth shut."

"I didn't do anything to Paisley!"

"Yes, you did. You had a fight with Sarah."

A fragment of the picture clicked together in my mind. Paisley's house after Sarah's funeral. "You mentioned a bruise on Sarah's stomach. I didn't know about it."

He nodded patronizingly. "It took her awhile, but Paisley figured out I shouldn't have seen it. She started thinking. Then talking. And she had the audacity to question me. ME."

"But you did it. She was right."

"She shouldn't have doubted me."

"How'd you get Maggie to go somewhere with you?" I hadn't thought to warn Maggie to avoid my friends. I should have.

"Your parents put her in a cab to school. I followed her and told her you wanted to see her. She hopped right into Gin's Jeep."

Please let a security camera pick that up, I thought. "I'm pretty sure the police will think you stole Gin's Jeep, by the way." Benji smiled, and it was an echo of Alex's wicked smile a while back. But this look chilled me to the bone.

"You're going to be the perfect fall guy."

"No way you can pin this on me."

"Angry Harper finally cracked. I can see the meme all over social media. You'll go viral like the cancer you are."

"I underestimated you," I said, barely stopping myself from pointing out that cancer isn't a virus.

"I'm used to it." There was an incongruent humor in his voice— black humor—and I stored that detail for later.

"Alex is so cocky that he's easy to persuade," I continued. "He wouldn't even notice. Our parents, our teachers, think you're so earnest. Slightly geeky, easy to forget."

"They'll feel sorry for me when this is over. So. Any last requests?" His tone mocked me.

"Nah, I'm good." I gave him my own half smile.

He narrowed his eyes. "You might have been able to handle Alex, Harper. But you can't charm me. You have no power here." Benji motioned toward the building. "Your biggest weakness is your sister."

I stared at him, trying to analyze his weaknesses like I did when sizing up players on the other team during soccer games. Did he move faster to the right than the left? He looked like a werewolf in puppy-dog clothing.

"Toss the phone to me," Benji said. He patted the pocket of his cargo pants; it looked like he had something heavy inside. "If you called anyone you weren't supposed to, you'll regret it."

I tossed him the phone. He bobbled it awkwardly before wrapping his fingers around it.

"Alex would have caught it cleanly," I said. "I guess coordination only followed one branch on the family tree."

No reaction. He glanced up and down as he tapped on the phone, presumably reading the call log and texts. I inched backward, hoping it was slow enough that Benji wouldn't notice. "Good girl," he said as he put the phone in his pocket. "Now stop moving." Benji pulled a gun out of his pocket.

I froze and put my hands in the air, but then dropped them. "Really? You're going to shoot me?" If I understood his plan, he'd never do it. He couldn't let it look like a murder. My heart started racing even faster. My hands felt shaky and I wanted to do something. Fight back. Think, Harper.

"Nah." Benji's smile made feel like bugs were crawling over me again, but I held my shoulders straight and stared at him. "You're going to shoot yourself."

THIRTY-TWO

TUESDAY MORNING, CONTINUED

"No I'm not," I said.

"Maggie is dead if you don't."

"Who do you think you're talking to, Benji? You'll kill Maggie if I shoot myself." A shadow moved in the woods. I hoped it wasn't Maggie. She'd better be working her way out of the park. Getting to safety.

"I need you to write a suicide note. Be sure to confess to killing Sarah and Paisley. I left your laptop on the table on your back porch. I'm sure the police will be fascinated by how you ended up with all sorts of private photos and files from Gin's parents. Especially since you posted the photos online earlier today with the username SoccerStar13."

A stick crunched in the forest behind us. Benji wheeled around, holding the gun in the direction of the noise. Two squirrels ran through the clearing.

As soon as Benji's back was to me, I vaulted through the air, driving my shoulder into his back. He fell to his knees and then tried to jump up and ended up on one knee, half-twisted to face me. The gun dropped into the dirt in front of him.

I kicked at his head as hard as I could, but my boot glanced off the side of his face as he ducked. He reached for the gun, so I stamped on his hand and kicked the gun away. He grabbed my ankle and dragged me to the ground. He punched me in the eye, and red lights burst around me.

He grabbed my neck with both hands and rolled so he was on top of me. I clawed at his hands, digging my fingernails in deep, trying to do anything to breathe.

A shadow came up beside us and crashed against Benji, knocking him off me. He rolled and grabbed the shadow, pulling it down to the ground with him with a flash of red.

I gasped but didn't have time to take in more than a breath. I rolled over, crawled a few feet, and grabbed the gun. I pushed myself to my feet, trying to see straight.

Benji was on top of Maggie, and she fought against him as he tried to wrap his hands around her neck like he'd done to me. I rushed forward and brought the gun down on the side of his head. He slumped over. I shoved him, one hand on his hip and the other on his shoulder, as Maggie rolled out from under him.

I stood over Benji for a second before winding up and kicking him in the ribs, but he didn't move. I couldn't make myself lean over and touch the artery in his neck to see if his black heart was still beating. Maggie gasped for breath beside me with her hands on her knees.

I pulled the phone out of the pocket of his cargo pants, my nose wrinkled as I touched his hip. I scooted back a few feet, holding the gun at my side in case Benji was just playing possum, although I didn't think so.

I looked at Maggie, who was still staring at Benji. I waved to get her attention.

"You okay?"

She nodded. One of her eyes was watering and was already bruising. She'd have a shiner tomorrow. I swallowed hard. A black eye is a much better fate than what could have been.

Get ahold of yourself, Harper. I took a deep breath and looked down at the phone.

I dialed 911.

"You need to send the police to Dry Hollow Park. I think I killed someone."

THIRTY-THREE

SEVERAL MONTHS LATER: JULY

Orange really isn't my color, and scrubs aren't my style. But something told me my prettiness factor was the last thing from Gin's mind as we sat at the plastic picnic table during visiting hours. My brother had already been by; he visits every week. Maggie writes me letters. Every day. The one time my father visited, he'd explained my mother's absence by saying that visiting me in juvenile detention was too much for her. She'd gone to a resort to relax and get away from it all. Right. Just like how I'm going to win Miss Congeniality in the annual Miss Teen Pageant, prison edition.

Daniel told me the truth: she'd gone to rehab. Finally. One that sounded like a day spa and offered massages. A good use for my college funds, I thought. I'm sure my father has figured out a way to pin that on me too. Just call me the destroyer.

We'd spent our visits talking about the future. Daniel reminded me almost every week that since my plea agreement had involved me being charged as a juvenile, my slate would be clean once I turned eighteen. I wasn't even technically a criminal; I'd been "adjudicated" through family court. For now, I'm just a delinquent, and he was full of information about how I could get my record sealed. We could go to a state college together, him as a transfer student from the community college where he was currently taking classes and me as a traditional freshman. If I wanted, I could even try to walk onto the soccer team. He didn't even care that I'd let him take the fall for the burglary at our house. He'd just waved his hand and said he couldn't blame me for a few bad decisions when his outnumbered mine. We'd yet to decide who had made the stupider mistakes, although I know the answer. Me.

I liked to listen to Daniel dream, and who knows? Maybe it would all come true.

But now I was looking at someone else who had his own dreams for the future.

About half of the tables were in use, with prison personnel stationed around the perimeter of the room.

"I'm glad my counselor gave you approval to visit," I said.

"My father says hello." Gin flashed me a half smile rimmed in sarcasm. "He finally appreciates you. Not that he wants me to date you."

I glanced around and made sure no one was in earshot. "About time. I'm glad my sacrifice made one person happy."

"I appreciate it too. I can't tell you how much. I should be in here with you."

"No, you didn't do anything as bad as I did. Stay outside with a clean record."

"I stood by for the first burglaries."

I'd left Gin's name out of everything I'd sent to the detective, and I'd consistently denied he'd been involved at all. I heard from my lawyer that Gin's lawyer wouldn't let him answer any questions. He'd said since there wasn't any evidence tying Gin to the burglaries, he wouldn't be charged. The lawyer tried to get me to roll on Gin to bargain for a reduced sentence. That's when I tried to fire him. He hadn't brought up Gin again.

"But you didn't know about me burglarizing Marisa Foret's house until after. Don't worry about it, Gin. Really. It makes me happy to think about you living your life. Even if I ruined mine."

"It's not ruined."

"I don't want you to wait for me," I said.

His words made me feel like we were in a cheesy B movie. Soon he'd be singing songs about how I was the only girl he'd ever wanted, and he'd knit a row on a blanket each day I was away so we'd have something to warm ourselves with when I rejoined society as a contributing member. The thought made my stomach grumble. "I'll be in here for a while. Feels like an eternity."

"Chin up. My dad said you could be out in a few months.

He followed your case closely, especially the negotiation over you pleading guilty," Gin said. "Harper, I love you. I want to wait. Graduation is barely a year away. With good behavior, you should be out by then."

I shook my head. "You're going to be moving forward, living. I'm figuring out which haircut goes best with orange." Gin's eyes were sad, not unlike Murphy's when he really wanted to go for a walk but no one would take him.

"Do you, you know, actually love me? Or were you just with me because I was always there?"

I studied the gray plastic tabletop for a moment before looking up and staring into Gin's brown eyes. "Do you even have to ask?"

Gin's eyes were sad. "I'm still driving Maggie to school and to her soccer games. She deserves to have someone cheering for her. Daniel makes sure she gets to practices and goes out with her friends."

I smiled. "She told me that in her letters. Thank you." When Maggie wrote that Gin had stepped up for her, I'd gotten my first full night's sleep since everything started a few months ago.

We sat in silence for a few seconds. "Gin, thanks so much for visiting. I miss you."

"I wish I could kiss you," he said.

I half smiled. "Not in here. Not allowed."

"Oh, I was given very clear guidelines. I'm surprised you haven't already broken a few while we've been sitting here."

"Not a good idea," I said. "Rule number one: the guards don't take shit from anyone. Follow the rules, or else."

Gin rubbed his eye like he was trying to stop a tear from escaping or something. "I don't want to leave you here."

"You have to."

"Can I bring you anything?"

"You know you can't." My voice was gentle. "Gin—"

"Visiting time is over," a guard said from behind me.

I stood. "Say hi to Maggie for me," I said, and I signed "I love you but you shouldn't visit again" before walking away. I didn't look back.

ACKNOWLEDGMENTS

For the past several years, I've been lucky to be part of a wonderful community of writers. I'll thank you in person, but I also want to mention you in my debut novel and say I'm glad you came on this adventure with me. Presented here in alphabetical order, with fingers crossed that I remembered everyone:

Shelby Bach, Jennifer Bosworth, Marla Bowie, Teri Brown, Laura Byrd, Bill Cameron, Miriam Forester, Robin Herrera, Amber Keyser, Fonda Lee, Susan Hill Long, Laura Marshall, Kristina Martin, Nadine Nettmann, Lisa Nowak, Jenn Reese, Heidi Schulz, Lisa Schroeder, Mary Elizabeth Summer, Chris Struyk-Bonn, Sonja Thomas, and Cat Winters. Also, a shout-out to Mark Vanderzanden for his help brainstorming screen names that would appeal to teenage basketball players. I've left two friends off the list above, as they need extra-special recognition: Kim Winternheimer and Nevin Mays. If writing is a marathon, not a sprint, they must feel like ultra-marathon support staff by now. They've read all of my work and celebrated my successes with me while offering pep talks when needed. I'm lucky to have both of you in my life.

Thank you to my editor, Ellen, at Poisoned Pen Press, and the crew at Sourcebooks Fire, for taking a chance on me and Harper. Last but not least, thank you to Jim, as none of this would have been possible without you.

ABOUT THE AUTHOR

Kelly Garrett's debut novel, *The Last to Die*, was a 2018 Oregon Book Awards finalist. When not writing, Kelly spends her time hiking with her Great Pyrenees mix and seeking out new coffee shops. After growing up in a small, rainy town on the Oregon coast, Kelly now calls Portland home, where she organizes several literary-related lecture series. She's an alumna of Pacific University. You can track her on Twitter @garrett_kelly and on both Instagram and Facebook @writerkellygarrett, or stop by and visit her at garrettkelly.com.

FIREreads

#getbooklit

Your hub for the hottest young adult books!

Visit us online and sign up for our
newsletter at FIREreads.com

 @sourcebooksfire

sourcebooksfire

firereads.tumblr.com